Mall Rats

Also by Kevin Robinson

Split Seconds

Mall Rats

A STICK FOSTER MYSTERY

Kevin Robinson

Walker and Company
New York

This book is dedicated to my friend Phil "The Fonze" Errion. When I first lay broken and scared in a Florida hospital room, wondering how I could ever survive without the use of my legs and my fingers, Phil spent many of his lunch hours at my bedside explaining it to me. Then, when I was finally released from the hospital, he introduced me to his fellow wheelchair athletes, and through them to much of Orlando's "disabled" community . . . most of whom were surviving quite nicely, thank you.

All the characters and events portrayed in this work are fictitious.

First published in the United States of America in 1992
by Walker Publishing Company, Inc.

Published simultaneously in Canada by Thomas Allen & Son
Canada, Limited, Markham, Ontario

Library of Congress Cataloging-in-Publication Data
Robinson, Kevin.
Mall rats / Kevin Robinson.
p. cm.
ISBN 0-8027-3215-1
I. Title.
PS3568.O2892M34 1992
813'.54—dc20 91-39623
CIP

Printed in the United States of America
2 4 6 8 10 9 7 5 3 1

Acknowledgments

Many thanks to all of the old and new friends who helped me get my second Nick Foster mystery off the ground and into the bookstores. Special thanks to:

Janet Hutchings, for buying and believing in *Mall Rats* in the first place.

Michael "The Sideman" Seidman, for enthusiastically adopting this poor orphan when Janet became editor of *Ellery Queen's Mystery Magazine*.

Bob Albright, for his tireless first reading and for insights that were unfailingly intuitive and subtle.

Officers Jeff and Barbara Roland, for being the cutest and most helpful Mom & Pop Cop team I know.

Sergeant Craig Sachau (U.S. Army), for answering all my questions . . . including the ones I didn't know enough to ask.

Bob Maine, Don Freidkin, and Brian Allman, for sharing their knowledge about firearms and ammunition.

Wayne Sarosi, for "gator-aide" above and beyond the call of nature.

The Friday lunch crowd (you know who you are), for, among so many other things, helping me open the saltine crackers.

▽

1

I HATE WEDDINGS, so I never go unless I have to. Tuxedos and wheelchairs just don't sit well together; and besides, I hate hanging out with people who appear altogether too happy. When that many men and women are all gathered in one place, smiling and handing out wishes for a blissful future, it's an unmistakable harbinger of doom. But this wedding was different. This wedding was mine.

Sitting on my own tail, and that of the rented tux, I could feel the flow of my perspiration change from seep to full cascade. Gray pinstripes look great with starched white shirts and electric blue ties and cummerbunds . . . but only on the store mannequins. And, as any astute mall goer knows, they never use seated display figures because a tuxedo is not designed to be worn bent in two different places. Perhaps this was intentional, a fitting tribute to the men who wear them—many of whom stand at attention for the rest of their lives.

Even my hardy companions looked out of place and restless in their brightly accessorized penguin garb. The three of them stood resolutely at my side, dwarfing me, of course, but also lending me great moral support. My friend and former housemate, Peter Stilles, was best man, and he rested his right hand firmly on my shoulder to remind me that I was not alone. Peter was like that. Then again, maybe he just wanted to be ready in case I tried to bolt for the side door.

Next to him, Stanley Fredericks rocked ever so slightly on the heels of his pointy-toed patent leather shoes. It wasn't primarily the fancy getup that made the tall, graying FBI agent uncomfortable—he wore a three-piece suit every day. But here, standing exposed in front of almost 400 people, Stanley was bereft of his standard-issue companion. The 10mm Smith & Wesson automatic pistol hung in its shoulder rig on the back of Pastor McClarrin's office chair. The book-lined study where we readied ourselves for the great performance at hand was just through the dark-paneled door behind us. Still, I knew that Stanley probably slept with the 12½-ounce Colt Mustang .380 auto he kept holstered to his left ankle. That weapon he would never leave behind.

At the end of our close ranks, my fellow newspaper reporter Todd Gulick stood staring into the fourth row. Even amid the colorful finery that filled the small Orlando church, Brenda "Butch" Grady's brilliant blue eyes stood out like beacons, gleaming at him with undisguised affection. I was startled to see how glamorous this athletic woman, who could clear a bar room or hit a softball into the next county, could look . . . when she chose to. To her credit, the formerly nerdy Todd looked the least out of place in his tuxedo. Butch spent months making the young man over, changing his wardrobe, his haircut, and, most of all, his sense of self-esteem. He impressed all of his friends, not to mention his coworkers at the *Melbourne Suncoaster,* where he had efficiently taken my place. Todd Gulick, rookie journalist, was a man on the way up.

As last-minute attendees were ushered to the few remaining seats, something or someone caught my eye; or rather, should have caught my eye but didn't really. The instant of recognition and loss was accompanied by a blurry flashback that spoke incoherently to my sense of smell . . . and then was gone completely.

Unlike most June weddings in central Florida, mine did not smell of fresh gardenias, orange blossoms, and mums. Oh, they were all there; the sanctuary had been beautifully decorated by Pam Ranger, who ran her own Orlando flower shop. But the unlikely aroma dominating the old Reformed Presbyterian church on Livingston Avenue and Broadway was that of Luigi Leone's homemade Sicilian sauce. Louie insisted on throwing us a dinner party reception, and the fellowship hall in the basement was now in his capable hands. There would, he promised, be pasta for all, as well as his famous "original New York style" pizza for the younger guests. Louie even made the cake.

And then there were the so-called mall rats. The regular parishioners, I'm sure, were unsettled by these young men and women who, in their nylon jackets, ripped sweatshirts, and spandex miniskirts, jammed the rear pews. The congregation must also have puzzled over the many familiar faces—faces that brought to mind neither names nor recollections of where they had been seen before.

That's the way it is with the people we see at the great sprawling shopping malls. Even the infrequent shopper sees them pushing trash bins or mop buckets, patrolling with radios clipped to their belts, or, in the case of the pubescent mall rats who flock there to escape the summer heat and the boredom of prejob-age school vacations, just "hanging out."

We usually don't even take time to learn the store clerks' names; and if we see one of them on the street, we might notice the familiar face, but we cannot quite place it. My latest month-long "Stick Foster Report" for the *Orlando Sentinel* (my new employer) was about mall life. It was being carried by a number of state and national papers—including my alma mater in Melbourne—so at least my readers and I were starting to take a second look at the nameless ones we had walked thoughtlessly by so many times before. Though I'd hardly made heroes of the men and women who kept the shopping cities alive and breathing, they seemed to appreciate being noticed.

But those gathered in the packed Orlando sanctuary—even the young and restless mall rats—didn't study each other for long. Throughout the crowded bench seats and the side aisles lined with orange ultralight wheelchairs (the Orlando Orange Wheels wheelchair basketball team was there in force), everyone's eyes quickly followed the handsome pastor's lead, and turned toward the back.

Because it was the small congregation's practice to sing a cappella, an organ had been brought in just for the occasion. Brad Ranger, the church's choir director, taught piano and organ and performed professionally. His customized processional filled the sanctuary, making temporary believers out of even the most cynical singles. When he had us in the palm of his talented hand, the bridesmaids filed down the center aisle, two of them in orange wheelchairs. Then Samantha Wagner, Esquire, positively stole the show.

Was I making a mistake? Had I rushed into this, pushing an incredible woman into a commitment she was not yet ready to make? If my lawyer bride ever wanted to eat my lunch in divorce court, I'd go hungry for sure. But in that moment, seeing Sam roll down the aisle on the arm of her brother, Jerry, it just didn't matter. Her long, golden hair swept in and out of the delicate lace like sunshine breaking through pure white clouds. Sam's wheelchair was buried somewhere in the cascading linen, but even if it had been visible, no one would have noticed. Her plunging neckline was probably too low to suit the more conservative women of the congregation, but I suspected that every man in the room was holding his breath . . . just as I was.

Suddenly, it seemed, Jerry put his baby sister's arm in mine . . . and there was no backing out. Bob McClarrin smiled easily as he opened the small black Bible in his hands and gently removed the gold silk ribbon that marked the passage he had chosen for our nuptials. His polished walnut pulpit stood on the podium behind him, but even there on the sanctuary floor, Bob McClarrin stood a head taller than most of his audience—probably not unlike Saul, the first king of Old Testament Israel.

"We are gathered here together," he began, "in the presence of God—"

"Ahhhhh!"

A wailing scream rose from somewhere in the congregation behind me. These Scottish Presbyterians, I knew, were not given to loud amens or speaking in tongues, but perhaps it was one of the visitors. Bob glanced up briefly and pressed on.

"—to join this man, Nicholas Foster, and this woman, Samantha Wagner, in holy mat—"

"Owwahhhh!"

I silently prayed it wasn't some radical Pentecostal bent on healing all the poor "cripples" in the crowded auditorium. The cry, however, was followed by the thud of a falling body.

There was a localized commotion near the back of the church before murmurs broke out all over. Sam and I rolled our wheelchairs apart and turned to join Pastor McClarrin as he gazed back up the center aisle. Martha Galliger lay there on the floor, half in and half out the pew. Her face was bright red, her eyes bugged wildly, and she flung her arms around her head, battering them mercilessly against the base of the wooden seats. Several deacons hurriedly gathered her up and carried her out, while her younger sister, Constance, rushed by us on her way to the phone in the pastor's study.

"Bogus!" Danny Singer blurted out from the back row when the stricken woman went suddenly still in the arms of her ordained bearers. "I think the old lady croaked!" One thing about mall rats: they generally get to the point of things in a hurry.

"Ladies and gentlemen," Bob McClarrin's powerful voice rolled out across the disturbed congregation. Order returned as the assembly gave their attention once again to the front. "Let's pause here for a moment and pray for Miss Galliger." The room fell silent. "Our Father," he said as if addressing someone standing next to us, "we lay before you the present need of our faithful sister . . ."

It was some time later—after the ambulance sped away with the Galliger sisters and a church elder—that Bob McClarrin beseeched the congregation back into some semblance of decorum and Sam and I finally said we did. Fortunately, most of the guests had already indulged themselves on Louie's authentic Italian cuisine when the word came that Martha Galliger had indeed died. After receiving a phone call from the hospital, the wife of the elder who accompanied the aging spinsters reported that the woman's heart had all but burst. Constance, understandably, was taking it all badly.

"She insists that her sister was murdered," the talkative elder's wife whispered loudly. A group of anxious listeners huddled around her, hanging on her every word. "And, well, with some of the characters here today," she added, her eyes darting back and forth protectively, "who could blame her?"

Fortunately, the mall rats had taken their free pizza upstairs, plugged a heavy-metal tape into the sanctuary's public address system, and were having a party of their own. It was amazing that my young friends had darkened the door of a church at all; had they heard a suggestion that their appearance made them murder suspects, the phenomenon assuredly would never be repeated. Besides, the very idea that anyone would murder dear old Martha Galliger was ridiculous in itself.

"Well," Sam had said, grinning, as we finally shook the last hand and hugged the last well-wisher in the reception line. "Nobody can say we didn't make it entertaining."

"A day to remember," I agreed. "Can we get undressed now?"

"Stick Foster!" she said, her blue-gray eyes brightening with feigned shock and genuine lechery. "Can't you wait until tonight?"

"I meant get out of this formal stuff," I said, shaking my head in mock reprimand, "but a mind in the gutter is a terrible thing to waste. What about the nursery . . . is there a lock on that door?"

"Don't you wish. Anyway, we've still got to cut Louie's cake."

We cut the cake, mingled until we couldn't stand it anymore, thanked all concerned, and hauled the loot back to our new Goldenrod apartment. Then we left for Miami, and a four-day honeymoon cruise around the Caribbean. It wasn't until we arrived home on Wednesday night that we learned Martha Galliger had indeed been murdered.

▽

2

"IT WAS LIKE a drug dealer's milkshake," Stanley Fredericks told me over the telephone. "The crime lab says there was enough crack, PCP, and amphetamine in Martha Galliger's bloodstream to kill a circus elephant."

"How was it administered?" I asked, shaken at the ramifications of Stanley's news.

"She drank it. Probably with the punch."

"She *made* the punch, Stan. And nobody else noticed anything."

"I know that, but the fact remains: there wasn't anything in her stomach but wedding punch and a boatload of controlled substances."

"Mm."

"And there's more, I'm afraid," Stanley added with some hesitation. "Someone stole my 10mm while we were downstairs making merry. I went up to change out of the monkey suit about half an hour after you and Sam took off, and there was just my empty shoulder rig hanging on Bob's chair with the extra clip still attached. I questioned a few of the church folk, but most everyone was gone."

"Any ideas?"

"What do you think?"

I didn't want to say what I was thinking. Stanley let the silence go on for a while and then said it himself.

"Your mall rats were up there the whole time, weren't they?"

The honeymoon was far from over, but Thursday sent Sam back to her new office at Ketchum, Latham & Bennet (Rodney, Rosemary & Robert—we called them "the three R's") and me back to my newly enhanced story at the Palmetto Plaza Mall. Under the disapproving eye of Leonard Gordon, the mall's security chief, I was swamped at the food court entrance by a sea of mall rats.

"Hey, Stick Man," said Danny Singer, grabbing the back of my chair, throwing me helplessly into a wheelie, and running me ahead of the herd, back toward their turf in the southeast corner of the fast-food multiplex. "Did ya hear the news? Somebody aced that old lady at your wedding."

"Yeah," said Billy "Bart" Simpson, "and the cops been askin' us all kinda questions . . . like we aced her or something. I don't think so."

"Like, I'm really sure," said Jeremy "Geek" Palmer. The poor boy's glasses were far too large for his head. "And that FBI guy, he thinks we took his gun."

"It's extremely bogus, I must say," added Emily Warner, tipping up her fuchsia sunglasses for emphasis.

"Totally," echoed several others.

If nothing else came from my interviews with those kids, at least I had finally learned a second language. I called it "awesomese."

What amazed me most was how different they were . . . and how much they were exactly the same. I've never seen one person—no, I've never seen twenty people—wear as many colors as Emily Warner. The brown-eyed, black-haired thirteen-year-old wore so many layers and so many Day-Glo colors that watching her walk made me dizzy. And somehow, her makeup always outpaced her clothing. She was brash, independent, and able to handle herself easily among the male-dominated pack. But when I interviewed her alone, sitting in the warm light of the big plate-glass windows that looked out over the parking lot to the Old Portico Restaurant and Colonial Drive, I caught glimpses of the lonely girl who was totally out of step with her family and her world.

Emily's body was changing, as young women's bodies of that age are wont to do; but sadly, she had no one—not even an older sister—to talk to about it. The changes swept her along, leaving her to sort them out for herself, or worse, interpret them through the filter of the other mall rats' coarse conversations. If she were not already sexually active, I knew it probably wouldn't be long. Yes, I know I was getting personally involved with my story, but I can't see how any caring person could spend time with these kids without seeing the potential and grieving the waste.

"Like, if we were going to kill somebody, you know," she said, pushing Jeremy out of the way and sitting down next to me, "we would do an old woman instead of Big Lenny."

Her joke brought laughter from her peers, but I found it strangely disquieting. "Big Lenny" was Leonard Gordon, and there was no love lost between these teenagers and the overweight mall security chief. If he could have legally thrown them all out of "his" mall, or better yet, "locked them all up for good," he'd have done it long ago. And every one of them knew it.

Inside, each wore various and sundry rejections like faded rock posters on the walls of their hearts. True, several of the other summer mall rats were flat-out bad kids; they did drugs, stole when they thought they could get away with it, and didn't know or care where the truth ended and the lies began. But these were basically good kids with nowhere else to go. Their loose summertime confederations took the place of real friends, real family ties, and real life.

"I could ace Big Lenny myself," Bart boasted. "And maybe I will."

"Bart, like you're such a fart," Emily said.

"Chill, Bart," Danny said, reaching over and pulling Bart's black Motley Crue hat down over his eyes. "Ya don't need ta kill Big Lenny . . . he's gonna die of a fat overdose any day now."

"Hardening of the arteries," Jeremy clarified. "You know, cholesterol."

My time with Billy "Bart" Simpson had been the most

troubling. The smallish but slightly pudgy fourteen-year-old with ragged blond hair and tattered clothing wanted desperately to impress the others, but beneath his bravado, his self-esteem was nonexistent. Billy lied pathologically, anything to impress a listener with his supposed worldliness and wide-ranging experience with life. He had never said so, but I strongly believe he was—before his father walked out on his mother—a physically abused child. Now, in the beginnings of what would likely be a seriously arrested adolescence, he showed a diminishing grasp of reality. Violent comics, videos, and movies were staples of his young life, and academics were only mildly more appealing than the thought of a grisly death. Billy's future didn't look at all promising.

"The token machine's screwed up again!" It was Wallace Jackson and his faithful shadow. "Yo, Rollin' Homeboy!" he said noticing me in the midst of the crowd. "Some wedding, eh?" He made a fist, waited for me to follow, and we hammered them together top and bottom. He and his little sister, Tamara, were the only black members of the Palmetto Plaza summer mall rats' association, and their big advantage over the rest of the group was their own close-knit relationship. They were eleven and fourteen years old, respectively, and through a half-dozen foster homes, Tamara and Wallace had clung to each other unfailingly. Sometimes a little family goes a long way.

"It's givin' seven or eight tokens for a dollar," Wallace added. "Come on!"

The rat pack rose around me as one, and rushed off toward the video arcade. They all knew divine providence when they saw it. Several of them reached out to touch me approvingly as they left.

"Later, Stickmaster," Danny said.

" 'Bye, Stick," Emily said, letting her hand brush across my shoulder as she hurried off with the others.

To listen to them talk about adults in general, and then to gain their approval, was strangely moving—a sensation that touched me deeply. And, unlike most "grown-ups," the mall rats weren't the least put off by my wheelchair.

"You're cool," Danny had pronounced the first time I addressed the group, trying to explain what my newspaper story would be about. "I accept you."

And that was all there was to it. It was better than a secret handshake. When I tried to explain it all to Sam, she just laughed and started calling me Peter Pan. Still, she promised to come one Saturday and meet the gang in their own surroundings . . . especially Emily Warner.

"Next," she'd said jokingly, "you'll be forming a new chapter of Big Brothers and Sisters."

Couldn't hurt. . . .

▽

3

AS FAR AS the unsuspecting shopper was concerned, I was hard at work. I'd been wandering the mall for a couple of weeks, chatting with regulars, conducting interviews, and setting up my scratched laptop computer on a food court table by the window. It was a pleasant place to work, after all. Outside, to the south, traffic on Colonial Drive moved east and west through Orlando. Below me, parking lot vultures circled in an unending hunt for the closest place to leave their cars. Around me on all sides, shoppers came and went, pausing at the food court to choose from one of over a dozen specialty fast-food shops. Their conversations, the voices of their youngsters, and the unending shuffling of metal and fiberglass chairs filled the well lit, highly polished indoor café with a cacophony of twentieth-century rhythm.

When they saw me tapping away at the small keyboard, they naturally assumed that Orlando's hottest new newspaper man, Nicholas "Stick" Foster, was working on his next report. Or maybe another story like the one I'd done in Melbourne, exposing the NASA computer saboteur and saving Disney World from a runaway Excaliber rocket. I appreciated the lifetime pass awarded me by the theme park's grateful and publicity-conscious management, but the whole story sort of grew in the telling. Even after a year, it was a hard act to follow.

No, instead of anything so grandiose, I was daydreaming

about my first Caribbean cruise. Actually, I don't remember much about the Caribbean. I don't even remember that much about the cruise ship, except that our wheelchairs wouldn't fit through the cabin door. (We transferred to the floor and scooted over the elevated threshold before folding the chairs and pulling them in after us.) But four days and nights, most of them spent sharing love with Samantha Wagner-Foster, wasn't a recollection easily pushed aside. There was no secret about who had been teaching whom, but if Sam objected to my inexperienced touch, she certainly never let on.

"Hello, Mr. Stick."

"Hello, Charlie," I said, dragged reluctantly away from my heavenly reverie.

"How do you make the words and look out the window at the same time, Mr. Stick?"

"Well, Charlie," I answered the diligent and insightful food court worker, "sometimes I can't. Sit down and visit for a while."

"Oh no, Mr. Stick. I don't get a break until"— Charlie's thick eyebrows bunched up with effort as he studied the hands on his big watch— "another sixteen minutes. Can I take this?" he said with a smile, pointing at the cup that I had long since drained of my morning coffee.

"Sure, Charlie. Thanks."

"It was a pretty wedding, Mr. Stick," he said as he started away with my refuse. "I'm sorry about the poor sick lady. Did she drink the bad drink, Mr. Stick?"

"Yeah, she did, Charlie," I said. "And thank you again for helping with the dinner. You did great." Charlie's wonderful smile got even bigger, and his enthusiastic nod told me that I was welcome.

There is an unmistakable magic about folks with Downs syndrome. Once upon a time they were shuffled off to institutions, believed to be incapable of learning. Today, thankfully, men and women like Charlie Martin are getting better educations, holding down jobs, and proving to the world around them that the value of human life cannot be measured by a preschool intelligence test. Sometimes, when I watched Charlie clean off the food court tables or mop up the red-tiled floor, I couldn't help wondering if the only higher order trait he had really missed out on was guile.

"Talking to old mud-for-brains again, eh, Stick? Learn any nuclear physics?"

Guile was something Leonard Gordon had in spades. The security chief turned a chair around, straddled it, and sat facing me with his meaty elbows on the table.

"In a lot of ways, Lenny," I said, trying hard not to show my anger, "Charlie's a lot smarter than you and me put together."

"Sure. And I'm the vice president."

Mm.

"What can I do for you, Lenny?"

"Well, I've been thinking about that lady at your wedding, Stick. I just know one of those delinquent mall rats did her in. Who else would be carrying that much dope?"

"I don't know, Lenny, but why would one of the kids want to kill an old lady they'd never met before?"

"Why do they do any of the criminal things they do?"

"What criminal things?" I asked. "They draw on the bathroom walls, Lenny. It's the best thing in there."

He didn't find me at all humorous.

"They've got no respect for anybody or anything. It's vandalism . . . that's what it is. They oughta be locked up—all of them."

"No, Mr. Gordon," said Luigi Leone, coming up behind him and making an eye-rolling face for my benefit. "It's their low-life, lazy, good-for-nothing parents who should be locked up. Children can't be expected to learn respect from television. That's where these kids grew up, in front of the television. When I was a boy in Sicily—"

"Not another holy homeland story," Lenny said, pushing his considerable bulk up off the chair and dismissing us with a wave of his fleshy hand. "I'm not sitting around here for another rerun of Gangster Island."

Luigi's neck reddened, but he refused to be baited. He took the big man's chair, turned it back around, and sat down.

"Da plane!" Lenny said, pointing at an imaginary horizon

as he waddled off. "It's da plane, Godfather!"

Luigi, who couldn't legally light up while spinning pizzas and ladling marinara sauce, made up for the smokeless hours by chain-smoking through his infrequent breaks. He exhaled a filthy cloud at Lenny's back, and if looks could kill . . .

"He's not worth it, Louie," I said. "I bet his own dog would bite him if it thought it could get away with it."

That made the wiry Italian-American laugh. "Yes," he said, his eyes brightening. "Gordon bitten by his own dog. That's good, Nicholas; you have to put it in your book."

"Maybe I will, Louie," I said, thinking it too real for the fantasy novel I had finally gotten around to starting on the side. "By the way, thanks again for the wonderful wedding feast. Everybody said it was the best chow they'd ever had at a reception."

"That's because they're not Italian." Friendly pride showed on his face. The light dusting of flour in his wavy black hair made him look older then the forty-two years he claimed as his age.

"I suppose the police asked you a million questions about Miss Galliger," I said, trying to change the subject gracefully. "What do you think really happened?"

"I've been thinking about that," he said. "There were quite a few people coming and going, like I told the cops, but the real thing is the cup she used, don't you think?" He didn't wait for an answer. "I didn't think about that until after I talked to them, but there were just five of us working down there, and we each had a paper cup. Miss Martha got them for us herself . . . insisting that we keep track of them and not be 'wasteful.' Red, they were, with white circles on them."

Louie used his first cigarette to light a second, then crushed out the first one against the heel of his shoe. He paused, staring right past me, as if he were looking at a slide projection of the church basement.

"Miss Martha filled them all for us. Right out of the punch bowl. I told the police that. And I told them that I don't remember where she put hers. Charlie sort of carried his around with him, you know how he does. Ernest set his on the coat rack by the door, and mine was on the pass-through counter to the kitchen. I think Miss Constance might have just carried hers around too. She was doing place settings right up until we all went upstairs for the service."

"Mm. Did you all leave together?"

"I think so . . . well, no, now that you mention it, I started out with them, but went back to get my cup of punch. I mean, it was only a second."

Louie paused, his puzzled gaze dropping to the table as if some lost clue were written there.

"So you got your drink?" I prompted him.

"No," he said, as if thinking of it for the first time. "It wasn't there."

▽

4

"WHERE HAVE YOU been?" Sam said from the bedroom. "Did you forget about Peter's party?"

"I'm sorry," I said. "I didn't forget. I just stopped at the police station on the way home."

"The Orlando police station isn't on the way home," she chided, rolling up alongside me and grabbing me by the hair that I had recently let grow out over the back of my collar. "Kiss me, you tardy fool."

Yes, ma'am.

We arrived at the out-of-the way south Melbourne marina a few minutes late, but Sam assured me that we were being fashionable. Neither of us had seen Peter Stilles's new yacht—neither of us could imagine how the young crabber could have afforded one—so we'd both been curious ever since the christening party invite arrived.

The marina parking lot was gravel and sand, but mostly sand. I parked my "new" car as close to the docks as possible. The black '86 Chevy Monte Carlo SS formerly belonged to Joe Stetler, player/coach of the Orlando Orange Wheels. He sold it to me after buying himself a white '88 with T-tops. "These are bona fide collectors' vehicles," he told me proudly. "Chevy made the last one in eighty-eight."

With the backseat removed, both of our folding wheelchairs fit nicely. We piled out into the warm coastal night, popped our front casters up out of the sand, and wheelied our way to the concrete sidewalk that ran along the water. By comparison, going up the steep wooden ramp to the docks was easy.

The main marina dock was nearly 50 yards long, and mooring lines from several dozen boats creaked against gunwales and cleats. The first yacht we came to was a great white beauty, at least 50 feet long, its upper deck adorned with potted evergreen and citrus trees. The slip number—as well as all common sense—said that it wasn't Peter's.

As it turned out, his yacht was not showcased near the front of the marina; in fact, if there had been any way to hide it altogether, I'm sure the management and most of the other tenants would have been delighted. Peter, however, positively beamed with pride.

"Ahoy, me hearties," he called out as we approached. "Arrh! 'Tis the plank for you, maties." And, indeed, Peter hauled a chunk of plywood out of the general rubble and used it to bridge the watery span between the dock and the disaster he had referred to in his invitation as a luxury yacht. When I paused uncertainly and motioned Sam to go ahead of me, she glared at me with suspicion.

"Got polite all of a sudden, didn't we?" Sam said under her breath as she rolled past me and out onto the makeshift span. It was disconcerting to notice that while the dock end of the plywood remained stationary, the ship's ancient decking slid back and forth under the other end, stopping each time a scant couple of inches short of dropping it off into the dark water.

"At least the tide's mostly out," Peter said with a smile. "A few hours ago, you'd have had to roll uphill to come aboard." He helped Sam onto the rear deck, where Butch Grady handed her a drink and Todd Gulick looked up from a marine patrol handbook on safe boating long enough to say hello.

Stanley Fredericks and his wife, Jennifer, waved their drinks at us, and Stan called out: "Don't worry, Stick. In case of emergency, your seat cushion may be used as a flotation device!"

"Thanks a lot, Stan," I said, rolling uneasily across the gently swaying bridge.

Once aboard, I looked around in dismay at the floating hovel. Words failed me. What do you say to someone who has clearly lost whatever good sense God gave him? But then Peter was from New York.

"It's a classic, Stick," he said, reading the disbelief on my face. "A thirty-five-foot Chris Craft with twin in-board Chrysler four-forties. She'll do better than twenty knots when she's running full out."

The concept that Peter's boat might actually go anywhere other than straight to the bottom of the marina was entirely too much of a stretch. The wheelhouse was draped in dirty canvas—either to keep out the weather or to protect the neighbors from the visual blight—and I couldn't even see the bow for all the debris. The deck, other than that section cleared for our gala evening, was strewn with scrap lumber, yellow electric cords, and empty caulking tubes. The only serviceable items above decks were the lawn chairs and the barbeque grill—all purchased, as it turned out, that very afternoon at the local K mart.

"Nothing but the best on this baby," Peter went on. "Teak, brass, you name it! I'm restoring her from stem to stern. I just moved in this afternoon."

"You *what?*" Everybody, including Peter, laughed at my incredulity.

"The rent's cheap, the neighbors are great, and I've even got pets," Peter said happily, delighted at having me on. He hopped onto the dock, picked up the freshwater hose affixed to the light post, turned on the tap, and let the stream splash into the salty marina alongside his boat. We all moved, albeit cautiously, to the port gunwale and peered into the dark water. In less than a minute, a massive dark form rose slowly to the surface, directly under the flow of fresh water. At first I thought it was Propjob, but the great creature had even more scars than the old dolphin that met Peter's crab boat each morning out on the Intracoastal Waterway.

"This lagoon is full of manatees," Peter said. "Sea cows, some people call them. The guy in the forty-footer over there showed me this trick; they come to the fresh water. Did you know that they're endangered?"

We all nodded.

"You sure don't see stuff like this in Endwell, New York."

After a christening feast of grilled steaks, steamed crab, and smoked mullet, Peter turned the floor—well, the deck anyway—over to me. "Okay," he said, "Stick's in charge of the evening's entertainment. In fact, he volunteered. But don't worry, if he bombs we can always crank this baby up and go out for a midnight cruise."

This last option clearly unsettled everyone, and they all looked at me with great expectation. And greater hope.

"This better be good, buddy boy," Sam muttered sternly. "I don't mind being called a shark, but I'm definitely not ready to become shark bait."

"If Peter even looks like touching the bowline, Stick," Stanley called from across the deck, "I shoot you first!"

Since that seemed to be the consensus, I pressed on with renewed vigor. "I've always wanted to go to one of those mystery dinners," I said. "You know, where the guests work through the clues and try to figure out who done it? Well, since we have a real mystery, I thought maybe we could try solving that."

"Sounds like work to me," Stanley said gruffly. Ever since receiving the official reprimand for losing his service weapon, Stan had been a little testy. It was a worse offense, even, than "kidnapping" civilians and allowing one of his government-issue Chrysler sedans to burn up on the banks of the Mosquito Lagoon and another to get blown up on Highway 50 east of Orlando. But that was past history.

"Nonsense," Jennifer said, hitting her husband with her elbow. "Stanley never talks about his cases, but I fancy myself a mystery fan. Have you read any Nancy Pickard?"

"Yes," I said, laughing, as Stanley rolled his eyes. "She does the Jenny Cain mysteries. Mm . . . So you can be Jenny Cain."

We spent ten minutes laughing and arguing about who would be whom. Todd, Butch insisted, must be Lord Peter

Wimsey. Peter Stilles proclaimed himself Inspector Clouseau—and, although there were several whispered votes for Stanley to play the bumbling sleuth, got his wish. Stanley chose to be Jim Rockford, and then suggested that I should be Chief Ironside. The blank stares from most of those present betrayed far too much about the difference between Stan's age and theirs, and he returned somewhat sullenly to his drink.

Butch clearly wanted to be V. I. Warshawsky . . . and who in their right mind would argue with either woman? For some reason it was decided that Sam and I should be Sister Steve and Father Dowling, and this seemed to amuse all hands. Okay, I can take a joke as well as the next guy.

"All right," I said finally, "you were all at a wedding where someone put drugs into a red-and-white paper cup filled with punch."

"Into Miss Martha Galliger's red-and-white paper cup," Stanley injected.

"Not necessarily," I said. "In fact, the drugs might have been placed in someone else's cup. Maybe one of three different cups." Now I had Stanley Fredericks's full attention.

"I never heard anything about that," he said.

"No, but I just stopped at the Orlando P.D. this afternoon, and the crime-lab folks say that traces of the drug mix were found in three cups."

I told them about the five people who had cups prior to the ceremony: Martha and Constance Galliger, Charlie Martin, Ernest Boyle, and Luigi Leone.

"Whose were the drugged cups?" Butch asked.

"Yes," Sam added, "and where were they found?"

"Good questions," I said, glad to see that my audience was getting caught up in the spirit of the chase. "We can only guess at two of them; waxed paper cups apparently don't fingerprint too well. But one of them was Louie Leone's . . . pizza flour leaves prints on almost anything. All three cups were found at the bottom of the wastebasket just inside the nursery door at the back of the sanctuary. By the time the police got the lab report and went to set up a crime scene, there'd already been two additional services at the church.

Fortunately, though, Ernest and Charlie were only supposed to clean up the downstairs fellowship hall, and the family whose turn it was to clean the building the next week was in Ohio."

"So," Jennifer said, one finger poised thoughtfully against her lips, "either drugs were added to three drinks, or drugged liquid from one cup drained into the others after they were thrown in the trash. Doesn't that make sense?"

"That makes lots of sense," Peter said. He sat over the hatchway, his long legs dangling above the stairs leading below decks. "But no one else experienced any effects of the junk, right?"

"Right," answered Stanley, obviously proud of his wife's observation. "That makes Jenny Cain's second scenario more likely."

Jennifer smiled.

"But do we know which cup was above the others?" asked Todd. "That would help."

"No we don't," I said. "We only know that the wastebasket was full of cups and paper plates, most of them probably from the kids who ate upstairs after the wedding. The three drugged cups were near the bottom."

"How many of the five original cups made it upstairs?" asked Butch.

"The police don't know, for sure," I said. "They do know the Galliger sisters both carried cups up, and that Constance showed Charlie the wastebasket in the nursery so he could throw his away. Beyond that, Ernest told them that he left his drink on the coat rack downstairs and retrieved it at the reception. Louie told me that he went back to get his so he could carry it upstairs, but it was gone."

"So his cup definitely ended up in the nursery," Todd summarized, "but he says he didn't take it there?"

"Right."

"Do we know who came and went through the fellowship hall while those five were getting things ready?" Sam asked.

"Only vaguely. Constance insists that some of the mall rats kept getting into things right up to the service; you know, sneaking bread sticks and sticking their fingers in the icing on the cake. Ernest didn't notice anything. And Louie says, yeah, he saw some of the kids, along with some church folks he didn't know."

"Hmmm . . . ," Jennifer said, looking disappointed. "It surely does look as if your mall rats are the chief suspects."

"Or at least one mall rat," Butch added.

"I know," I said. "That's what the police say too. But what if Martha wasn't the target at all? What if she picked up Louie's cup by mistake and drank from it on her way upstairs?"

"Well," Stanley said thoughtfully, "that would answer some questions. It's been my experience that a lot more Sicilians take hits than little old church ladies."

▽

5

THE NEXT MORNING I found Ernest Boyle in the hallway just outside the mall offices near the public rest rooms. He stood high on an aluminum folding ladder, his upper torso out of sight in the hole where one of the white suspended ceiling tiles had been removed. His heavily laden suede tool belt hung loosely around his waist, helping to pull his tan work pants even farther down over his skinny hips and nearly nonexistent buttocks. Looking up at him was safe enough, but it wasn't a pretty sight for passersby whenever Ernest had to squat on the job. There are clearly some cleavages God never intended mankind to show off.

"Hey, Ernest!"

"Why, hello, Nick," he said, straining to peer down at me. "What can I do for you?"

"Just talk, Ernest. Can I ask you a few questions?"

"Sure. About what?"

"About the wedding," I said, moving back to allow a young mother to push her stroller to the ladies' room. Between my wheelchair and Ernest's ladder, we pretty much blocked the whole hallway.

"Oh. Well, that was really too bad, so to speak, about the lady who died," he said. "Miss Martha, wasn't it? But I told the police everything I could remember. I'm glad there wasn't anything put in my cup, but then I kept track of it like she said, and put it up high, out of harm's way, so to speak."

"Yes, that was fortunate," I said. "Do you remember seeing anyone else downstairs before the ceremony?"

"Well, I was working, so to speak, setting up folding chairs and putting them 'round the tables there. I really didn't notice too much else." Ernest smiled down at me through the hole in the ceiling, then said as an afterthought: "Why, even old Pussyfoot told me to keep up the good work."

"Pussyfoot?"

"Yeah," he said, his chuckle echoing around in the overhead mechanical access space, "some of us call Mr. Gordon that 'cause he just sort of creeps around the mall, so to speak, you know, like a fat, sneaky old cat."

"Lenny? Lenny told you that? When, Ernest?"

"When I was putting up the chairs. He was just making talk, so to speak. You know how he does."

The men's room door swung outward and Danny Singer bounced out, almost running into Ernest's ladder.

"Whoa!" he said, replacing the cap on a black El Marko and looking up at the mall's head maintenance man. "Sorry, Soda Speak. I almost got you that time. Hi, Stick Dude. What's shakin'?"

"Palm fronds in the wind, Danny. What's up with you?"

"Nothin'. Ya know, the usual. Ya comin' up for lunch later?"

"Save me a place."

"Great!" he said, skipping down the hallway and disappearing into the mall.

"Quite a lad, that one," Ernest said. "You'd never know it, but I was a dickens like that once."

I heard a sharp snipping noise, and then a piece of red wire insulation fell out of the ceiling and onto my lap. "I'd have never guessed," I said. "Ernest, are you sure Lenny told you to 'keep up the good work'?"

"Why, of course. Oh, then, now that you mention it," he said without looking down at me, "I guess I did see someone, so to speak, didn't I?"

* * *

I passed Fred Lucas on my way back to the food court. He was posed thoughtfully in the entrance to Jacob's Clothiers, where he worked as a senior salesclerk.

"Hi, Fred," I said. "How's business?"

"Slow," he said, taking the bent-stemmed pipe from his mouth with one hand and caressing one of his black wool elbow patches with the other. "Summer is usually pretty slow. How was your honeymoon, Stick?" His left eyebrow—gray like his well-styled hair—rose, while a mischievous grin formed behind the aromatic cloud of pipe smoke.

"Too short," I answered, knowing that I was blushing under my beard.

"Anything new on the death of Miss Martha? She was such a hoot."

"You knew her, Fred?"

"Sure. She and Miss Constance have been coming here for years, almost always over Martha's objections. To watch them shop, you'd never know they were wealthy. They fussed over every purchase as if their Social Security checks were at stake. Sometimes they'd sit there," Fred added, pointing at the stylish bench seat on the concourse behind me, "and fuss for ten minutes before they even came in!"

"I knew they owned some land—"

"Some land! They say old man Galliger bought up thousands of acres out in Ocoee and Winter Garden after the Great Depression, planted most of it in citrus, and then left it all to his girls when he died in the late fifties. You know what's happened to land values out there since then."

"Mm."

" 'Mm' is right. Most of those new housing developments out off of White Road are sitting on old Galliger land, and you can bet Miss Martha and Miss Constance didn't give it away . . . *especially* if Miss Martha had any say in it!"

When I reached the food court, Leonard Gordon was towering over my mall rats, his neck bright red, and his forefinger waving threateningly. *My mall rats*. Funny how I'd come to see the core group of kids I had interviewed and gotten to know as *mine.* Maybe I really was turning into Peter Pan.

"Hey, Stickster," Danny Singer called out, "can ya tell this big gorilla to get off our case? We ain't done nothin'!"

"What's the matter, Lenny?" I said, rolling my chair around the big man and placing myself between him and the obviously agitated young people.

"Just a warning," he said, looking down at me with angry satisfaction. "Just a warning." He turned and stalked back into the mall concourse, his belt radio, cuffs, and nightstick bouncing like spastic planets orbiting his great girth.

Pussyfoot?

"What was that all about?" I asked.

"He's, like, crazy, Stick," Emily Warner said earnestly while rearranging the hot pink bandanna tied around her jet black hair. "He says one of us killed that lady at your wedding, and he's gonna prove it. I'm sure. Mostly he was looking at Bart."

Everybody nodded agreement—everyone but Billy Simpson. He just stared at the tabletop, with his jaw clenched. I caught the faint clicking sound of his treasured switchblade under the table.

"Put it away, Billy," I said. "Do you want people to believe him?"

"No," he said sullenly. His hand came out from under the table, then disappeared into one of the deep pockets in his surplus Desert Storm camo pants. "I hate his guts."

"Jeez, Bart," Danny said, "who doesn't? Chill out."

"Okay," I said, rolling up to the table and helping myself to Wallace's soft drink, "so what did Big Lenny say . . . exactly."

"He was awfully upset," Jeremy Palmer said. "More so than usual. Like, he was exhibiting all the classic signs of high blood pressure."

"The Geek's right," Emily added. "Big Lenny was, like, really stressed out, you know? Having a cow."

"He was shakin', man," Wallace Jackson said. "Like he was gonna lose it any minute."

"And spitting," added Tamara quietly. "It was too gross."

"Okay, I get the picture, but *what* did he say?"

They all just looked at one another in silence for a second, then turned to Danny. The sandy-haired pack leader spoke slowly. "I'm not really sure what he said, exactly. I mean, he was so freaked I didn't pay that much attention to what he was sayin' . . . just that he was talkin' about one of us killing Old Lady Galliger."

Everybody else nodded in agreement. It made some sense. But Leonard Gordon was the bully type; big, mean, and in control. Seeing him all red-faced and flustered had given even me a start. Not knowing what to make of it, and not wanting to further alarm the kids, I shrugged it off and changed the subject.

"Well, never mind. He's gone now. Here," I said, handing Jeremy a ten-dollar bill, "pizza's on me. Then I have a proposition for all six of you."

▽

6

GETTING MARRIED IS like switching to a precision sealed-axle bearing. Once you try it, you wonder how you ever managed without. In the old days, when all wheelchairs weighed over 80 pounds and the open bearings picked up every piece of dust, thread, and cat hair in the universe, pushing through life was really hard work. Living alone, I discovered quickly, had been hard work too . . . only I hadn't realized how much so at the time.

Coming home (the term had a whole new meaning) to Sam each night was a continuing adventure in joy. We told each other everything about our day, pored over wheelchair-accessible house plans, and made love. Nothing in my lifetime of reading, nothing in the scoring reports of my randier friends, and nothing in the steamiest scenes of the R-rated movies I had attended prepared me for real lovemaking.

"People have sex for lots of reasons," Sam whispered one night while I lay flushed and spent, staring contentedly at the myriad specks of the color blue in her eyes. "Sometimes it's for no better reason than to prove a point. I don't even know what the point is, exactly, but I did that a lot before I met you." She ran her fingers across my chest, up my throat, and through the hair on the nape of my neck.

"Thanks for reminding me."

"Oh, stop it. Anyway, this is what it's really supposed to be about."

I often wondered what sex would have been like before my spinal cord injury, sometimes wishing I hadn't been quite so chaste in the years just prior to falling off my dad's garage roof. It was hard to imagine anything better than my nights with Sam. "Sex is ninety-five percent in your mind and in your heart," a rehab counselor once assured me. "When those things are right, everything else is bound to be okay." I finally understood something of what she meant.

"So, what about Saturday?" I asked Sam as she nestled into my arms and showed every sign of drifting off. My brown Tonkinese cat, Butkis, always sensed this transitional time before I did and had already joined us on the big waterbed, curled up behind Sam's knees, and fallen soundly asleep. Traitor.

"Will it take you that long to get your strength back? I really am good!"

"You know what I mean."

"If the three R's don't need me, yes, I'll go."

All right!

Friday had all the makings of a zoo, but I was committed—or, perhaps, I should have *been* committed was more like it. Sam rolled over that morning as I was leaving, in fact, and woke up just long enough to say, "You're nuts." I pulled into the Palmetto Plaza parking lot at 4:00 A.M., half expecting no one to be there. But I was delighted to see all six of my recruits waiting anxiously by the main entrance. There wasn't a sleepy eye in the bunch.

"Hey, Stick!" Danny shouted. "We're here!"

"Like he didn't know that, dufus," Emily said. "I get shotgun!"

Jeremy was already reaching for the passenger door, clearly hoping to get the other bucket seat for himself, but hastily deferred to the brightly dressed woman-child.

"First, put my wheelchair in the trunk," I said, tossing the keys to Billy Simpson. "Emily, you'd better share the front seat with Tamara; those hooligans will be packed in pretty tight back there."

"Sure. Come on, Tam, let the *boys* sit back there on the floor!"

Tamara Jackson generally didn't talk much, but her smile was warm and intelligent and her dark eyes shone with perception well past her years. She let the guys pile into the backseat of the black Monte SS, jabbing her brother playfully in the ribs as he squeezed past, and then got in and scrunched up next to the car phone.

"You're in charge of the telecommunications, the stereo, and the stick shift," I told her seriously. "Put this baby in Drive and then find a good FM station."

Her pretty eyes got big, and she looked at the automatic transmission lever as if it might bite her if she made a mistake. Then, seeing the *D, D1,* and *D2* settings, she puzzled it out quickly and tugged at the stick. When it wouldn't budge she looked disappointed.

"Just pu—" Wallace said before I stuck my knuckles in his mouth.

"She'll figure it out just fine," I told him, casting a warning glance at the others.

Pride lit up her face as she pressed the button on the side of the shift handle and pulled the lever even with the *D* marking. "That one?"

"You bet." I peeled rubber in the empty parking lot and aimed the old Monte toward the coast.

It was crowded in the old wooden work boat. Two adults and six young people, when added to Peter Stilles's daily allocation of bait, brought the *Sea Shell*'s gunwales several inches closer to the water line, and the ancient 65-horsepower Mercury outboard protested ominously as we headed out of the south Melbourne marina toward the Intracoastal Waterway.

"Crank this baby up," Danny said, nudging me with his elbow. He stood next to the pilot's chair with one hand on the windshield, staring out into the dissipating darkness. "Let's see what she'll do."

"Can't you read?" Emily snapped. She sat behind us on the big white bait box. "The signs all say 'No Wake.' "

"Yes," Jeremy added quickly, "but we're already awake! Get it? Wake? *Awake?*"

There was an instantaneous chorus of boos. "Can't we throw him over for that, Peter?" I asked.

"Keelhaul him!" Wallace suggested. "That's what the pirates used to do."

"First time's a warning," Peter Stilles said with a laugh. "After that we'll make him walk the plank."

The on-the-job introduction to crabbing was a big success. Under Peter's watchful eye, they took turns hauling up the traps, emptying out the snapping blue crabs, filling the bait wells, and dropping the wire cages back into the water. One by one, I let them take the wheel, teaching them how to approach each trap and slow down just long enough for someone to grab the next buoy line. Their exuberance was infectious, and I didn't notice that there was one exception to the party spirit until I called Billy Simpson to take his turn as pilot.

"After we snag this next trap," I said, pointing to the blue-and-orange buoy on the water ahead of us, "take her back around to the north, up under the bridge, okay?"

"Sure," he said.

Something in the tone of his voice made me pay closer attention. The normally boisterous youngster was going through the motions, doing what he was told, but all was not well.

"What's up, Bill?"

"Nothing."

"Mm." Billy glanced over his shoulder as Tamara, leaning out across the water, scooped her hand under the buoy and grabbed the yellow nylon rope that connected it to the trap resting on the sandy bottom. "Got it!" she said, and Billy eased the throttle forward smoothly.

"How's that?" he said, turning the wheel and pointing the boat north. He didn't look at me, but I saw the glistening sparkle of moisture in his eye and heard the strain in his voice.

"Perfect, Bill," I said, slapping him on the shoulder. "Look, I didn't mean to bug you, but you're my friend. You can talk to me any time you want . . . or not at all. That's it, head between those two bridge pilings, and watch the cross current; it's wanting to push you to port. The next string is over there toward the east shore, just after we go underneath."

He got control of himself quickly, guided the old boat up the channel and under the bridge without a hitch, and headed for Peter's second string of blue-and-orange buoys. Emily was getting ready to take her next turn at pickup and I put my hand on Billy's shoulder.

"Let me take it for a minute," I said. "Grab a pogy and go stand next to Emily while she brings up that trap. You'll know what to do after that."

He gave me a puzzled look, but did as I had asked. "What are you doing, Bart?" Danny said, ruffling the smaller boy's blond hair as Billy reached into the bait box and then moved past him toward the stern. "Getting yourself a snack?"

"Some consider raw fish a delicacy," Jeremy observed. "The Japanese put it on rice and call it sushi."

The refrains of "Gross!" were quickly cut off, replaced by exclamations of wonder. Emily had caught the next trap line and was pulling it hand over hand out of the water but nearly fell overboard when a great gray form rose up nearly in her face.

"Awesome," Billy said quietly as the others squealed with delight. He held out the pogy and beamed as Propjob took it gently from his hand. The old dolphin slipped silently back, only to burst out of the salty water several yards away.

"I'll bet he did that on *porpoise!*" Wallace said, nudging Jeremy in the ribs. The others booed.

"Well, actually," Jeremy said, rolling his eyes at the pun, "that is an Atlantic bottle-nosed *dolphin* . . . and not a porpoise at all."

While the rest of the mall rats scrambled toward the bait box, digging hastily into the stash of dead fish, Billy just stood with both hands on the gunwale watching the watery ballet.

"Thanks, Stick," he said, without looking away.

"You're welcome, bud."

Back at the docks, after a lunch of delivered pizza, Peter put the mall rats to work on his luxury yacht. That was the deal, after all; they work for Peter on Friday; I take them all to Disney World on Saturday. So, while the portable stereo entertained every tenant at the south side marina, the enthusiastic kids took turns scraping old paint, sanding, caulking, and playing with the manatees. It wasn't professional help, but it was free. And Peter recognized the considerable value to all concerned.

▽

7

WE TOOK TWO cars out to Disney. The ladies, I was glad to see, wanted to ride in Sam's red Mustang convertible; and though I'm sure the guys wouldn't have minded Sam's company a bit, they remained loyal to me and piled back into the Monte Carlo. One of the many benefits of the day past was that I found myself gaining at least some ground with Billy Simpson. He faced down Danny Singer for the right to ride shotgun and appointed himself my personal attendant throughout our tour of the Magic Kingdom.

"Do we get into everything the back way?" he asked when we bypassed the long line into the famous Haunted House and entered through the dark portal clearly marked "Exit Only."

"Sure. Stick with Stick. First class all the way."

Later we split an order of fries by a window that overlooked the It's a Small World ride and waved to Sam and the rest of the mall rats when their boat went by beneath us. Sam's wheelchair sat empty on the platform, a reminder that she, at least, could not exit the ride elsewhere. The mall rats took turns holding our chairs whenever we transferred in or out, usually expressing some veiled threat to nearby Disney personnel that "they better still be here when we get back."

"I've been on that dorky ride," Billy had explained when we arrived at the Small World pavilion. "It's nothing but a bunch of dolls anyway."

I had nodded noncommittally and suggested a snack.

"Why do you think Big Lenny is on your case, Bill?" I asked between french fries, hoping the friendly mood of the day would hold through a few hard questions. He tensed up; his eyes darted like a cornered rabbit, but I pretended not to notice. Either he'd talk to me, or he wouldn't.

"I don't know."

He was lying. I took another fry and waved back at a youngster whose boat floated past below us. "Bill," I said evenly, "I'm not saying that you had anything to do with Miss Martha's death, but just between you and me, do you know anything about where the drugs might have come from?"

I watched his face in the reflection of the window while I waved to another boatload of exuberant tourists. He looked ready to bolt, but I acted like nothing was wrong. "I mean, if we could track the supplier—"

"Why does it always have to be me? Why couldn't it be somebody in that stupid church? I get blamed for everything!"

"Relax, buddy," I said, quickly putting a hand on his shoulder and looking him in the eye. "I'm not blaming you. Do you hear me? And yes, it could have been somebody in the church who killed Miss Galliger. But to prove that, it would help to know where they got the drugs, wouldn't it?"

Billy Simpson was a mass of nerves, writhing around in his seat like Jell-O in an earthquake. "Look, forget it," I said, fearing that I'd already pushed too hard. "I've just been wondering a lot about it, trying to figure it out. You're street smart, I needed some help, so I asked you. I've asked lots of people, so relax. Okay?" I went back to the french fries.

"Well, what did you think?"

"I think I'm tired and I want to take a bath." Sam took her nightshirt off and disappeared into the bathroom.

"I mean about the kids."

"We're *not* adopting the mall rats, if that's what you mean."

"Sam! No kidding. Aren't they neat?"

"Yeah, I guess they're not bad . . . as social misfits go." She closed the door in my face.

"Come on."

"Okay," Sam said over the sound of running water, "except for the one they call Bart, they're really not too bad. But you can't keep them."

"Bart? You mean Billy Simpson. What's the matter with him?"

"You're not that dense, Stick—though sometimes I wonder. Even if that boy had nothing to do with Martha Galliger's death—and it wouldn't surprise me at all if he killed her himself—he's headed for trouble . . . a time bomb waiting to go off. He gives me the creeps."

It bothered me to hear Sam say that—even if it was true. "What about Emily?" I turned the knob and eased open the door until it stopped against Sam's empty wheelchair. "Do you think she'll be okay?"

"I don't know what you mean by okay, but she's a tough little lady."

"I mean girl stuff, you know, not having somebody to talk to about . . . growing up."

Sam laughed loudly. "Did you collect stray cats and injured birds when you were a kid? I always knew you were the type. Look, babe, most girls don't have anybody to talk like that with. Lord knows I could never talk about sexuality with my mom. Your dad spoiled you, you know? I envy you having someone like that as a parent, but it's pretty rare in the real world. 'Girl stuff.' Sometimes you crack me up. Close the door; you're letting in a draft."

Well, there was no denying that I was new to girl stuff. The first time Sam sat in *our* bathtub and shaved her legs, I parked in the doorway and stared like an idiot. It was a scene so outside my experience that I pondered it for days afterward. When I asked Sam about it, she just laughed and said, "Somebody should have bought you a big sister when you were young."

Going to church wasn't new to me at all. My mom died when I was pretty young, but I still remember getting dressed up and going to church on Sunday mornings. The only thing that changed in the years that followed her death was that

Dad wasn't so hot on suits and ties, so we got a little more casual. I liked that a lot. But Dad wasn't a Sunday Christian. His faith was a day in, day out thing that permeated the way he lived his life.

"Son," he said often, "if God made this world—and I believe He did—then we ought to find out as much as we can about what He had in mind for us to do with it. There's no place quite like a good church to set about getting at that."

Dad would have liked Bob McClarrin's church. Dad would have liked Bob McClarrin. I don't quite know how the congenial pastor got us so involved—especially Sam—but before we knew it we were attending the small Orlando church, serving on various committees (I've always hated committees), and feeling very much a part of what Bob often called "the body."

On the morning after our excursion to Mickey Mouse's place, Bob preached on spiritual gifts. Each person, he told us, might have many talents, but also one special gift, given by the Holy Spirit. The tall and handsome preacher quoted I Peter 4:10, along with several supporting passages including I Corinthians 12 and Romans 12.

"This is part and parcel of who we are," he said. "It determines our very perspective on the world around us, like a lens though which we view the creation. Some even argue that our spiritual gift provides the motivation we need to be successful, effective human beings. Consider the list in Romans Twelve. This is, I believe, a comprehensive list of the *charismaton,* the 'variety of gifts' referred to in verse four of First Corinthians Twelve.

"Think about the people around you. Some of them are clearly leaders; we look to them without even thinking about it. Others are comforters; they just look us in the eye and seem to know when we are down and need a hug. Still others are servers who willingly take on those detailed, busy-work jobs that drive others of us crazy! The exhorter is, according to the Greek, *paraklesis,* or 'one who comes alongside.' Do you know someone who, whenever they are with you, always makes you feel like your friendship has real value? Or that they'll always be there to help you along if you should need them?

"We can all learn to be better in each of these areas," Bob went on, "but if God has specially gifted us in one of them, it effects the way we approach everything else."

I opened the pew Bible to Romans 12 and thought about the mall rats. Certainly they each had a "gift." Danny was clearly a leader, though he seldom bossed the others around. If Jeremy wasn't a teacher, I probably didn't know one. Emily was less obvious, but as I thought about her searching brown eyes and the gentle friendliness of her casual touch, I suspected strongly that she had a comforter's heart. Wallace could easily be an exhorter, and his sister, Tamara, was either a server or a giver. She was the group's "gofer," but more often because she volunteered then because she was asked.

Then there was Billy Simpson. I reviewed the seven gifts listed in the text before me, but pathological liar was nowhere in the Apostle Paul's inventory of the *charismaton*.

▽

8

THERE WAS A twenty-minute break between the main service and the Sunday school classes that followed. The kids used the time to stretch their legs and burn off some of the energy they had stockpiled sitting through Bob's sermon, while the adults gathered downstairs in the fellowship hall for coffee and doughnuts. I generally make it a point not to push my wheelchair through a crowd with a Styrofoam cup of hot coffee stuck between my thighs, but I wanted to talk to Constance Galliger.

"Miss Galliger?"

"Why, Mr. Foster. How are you this morning?"

"Fine, thank you. Why don't you just call me Stick?"

The look on Constance's face told me that she found that suggestion absurd. Okay . . .

"Sam and I wanted you to know how sorry we are about your sister. We certainly would have come to the funeral—"

"Nonsense," she said smartly. "If I'd had the choice between a honeymoon and my sister's funeral, I'd have chosen the honeymoon too. I think you showed great discernment in the matter."

The women with whom she had been speaking prior to my arrival chuckled. My naive fascination with girl stuff extended to elderly women too. Something about the nature of an old woman's cumulative wisdom always struck me as bordering on the fantastic, certainly rooted in the mysterious. Vague memories of my grandmother and a lifetime of semiannual visits with my dad's older sister, Vera, left me convinced that if all the things those ladies knew about life were ever set down in print it would shake the foundations of our supposedly male-dominated world. In fantasy there are wizards; in the real world there are older women.

"Well, thanks," I said for lack of anything more appropriate. "By the way, I've been following the police investigation, and I'd like to think they can eventually catch Martha's killer . . . even though it doesn't look very good right now."

"Thank you for your concern, Mr. Foster. I'm sure the police are doing everything they can."

"I was wondering," I said, trudging on, "if I might come out tomorrow and talk to you about the day of the wedding?"

Constance hesitated only an instant, then touched my arm the way older women seem to do and told me to come by for iced tea at around ten o'clock. The bell indicating that it was time for classes to begin rang twice; I thanked Miss Constance, and we all headed off to our various study groups. Sam and I attended the sermon discussion class led by Gene Woods, one of the church elders. I was anxious to learn more about this spiritual gift thing.

The old two-story house on White Road was the picture of southern charm. It was a whitewashed Victorian affair, probably built in the late thirties. An inviting covered porch stretched across the front of the Galliger home, replete with wicker fan-back chairs and bentwood rockers. Stately oak trees, draped in Spanish moss, braced the house on either side, but the rest of the expansive yard was planted in even and neatly cultivated rows of citrus.

I parked next to a healthy-looking grapefruit tree and pulled my wheelchair out of the Monte's backseat. There were four porch steps between me and the old front door, so unless I wanted to throw rocks at the doorbell button, I would have to rely on my own rude but effective calling method, the car horn. I settled into my chair, but before I could reach back to honk for Miss Constance, she swept out the front door and down the steps to meet me.

"Why, Mr. Foster," she said, pulling a light, beautifully hand-knit shawl around her shoulders, "how nice you could make it." Constance motioned for me to follow her around the back of the house. "The kitchen door is at ground level," she explained.

Her cotton print dress was obviously new, and probably expensive, and her blue canvas sneakers looked just like the ones Mr. Rogers takes out of his neighborhood closet every day. Fifty yards behind the old house, through a forest of scrub oak and palmetto, was a small, crystal clear lake with a white sandy beach.

"We grew up swimming in Fish Lake," Constance said, holding the kitchen door open for me. "Father had the beach sand hauled in by the truckload. There's always been a gator or two back there, but they seem content enough eating the occasional stray dog."

The kitchen was clean and tidy but surprisingly out of date. The cupboards were whitewashed and plain, the sink was an ancient cast-iron model, and the kitchen table was one of those white enamel-coated metal jobs that I had thought went out shortly after the dinosaur. Constance pulled a chair away to make room for me at the old table and went to tend a teakettle that hissed softly on the great white gas range against the back wall.

"I've been after Martha to remodel this old kitchen for years," she said over her shoulder. "A bit tightfisted, our Martha. I suppose there's no reason not to do it myself now." She poured the steaming tea over a converted jelly jar full of ice cubes, and the sharp cracking sound echoed off the metal tabletop. "Sugar?"

"Yes, thank you," I said, reaching for the white china sugar bowl. "I find it difficult to believe that anyone would deliberately poison your sister, Miss Galliger. Do you have any idea who might do such a thing?"

"The police asked me that too, of course. No, I can't imagine anyone hating her that much. Oh, she spoke her mind often enough at the CGA meetings—didn't always go with the flow, you know—but no one would kill her for that."

"CGA?"

"Citrus Growers Association. Father was a founding member, and Martha took his place when he died. She didn't take to the new big-business approach to marketing, and whenever they tried to hit the members up for higher public relations and advertising costs, she fought like a wildcat. I'll take her place now," Constance went on, "but it's all getting to be rather academic. Another bad freeze and there may not be any more Orange County citrus industry to promote."

"So I've heard."

"We've sold almost a third of our land to developers, and they're clamoring for more. If the weather in recent years hadn't been so bad, Martha would never have agreed to sell that much, but she spent a lot of the money buying and planting new trees to replace the ones we lost in the last three hard freezes. And it will be several more years before they start to produce . . . if they survive."

"What do you think happened at the wedding?" I asked before the conversation went any farther afield.

"Those kids," she said, her voice getting lower and harder. "Maybe they never intended to hurt anyone, but who else would have access to the kind of drugs that killed my sister?"

"I don't know, Miss Galliger. I just don't know."

▽

9

LUIGI LEONE WAS busy getting ready for the lunch crowd when I arrived at the Palmetto Plaza food court. While several teenage employees and two of his sons hustled around him, he gracefully spun a large round portion of pizza dough in the air over his head. There were more than a few floury skid marks on the off-white acoustic ceiling tiles.

"Hi, Louie. How's the cheese?"

"Fresh today," he said with a wink. He let the pizza dough drape limply over one wiry arm while he scooped up a handful of freshly grated mozzarella and passed it to me across the shiny stainless steel counter. "What are you writing today, my friend?"

"The great American novel, Louie. What do you think?"

"I think you can do it, Stick," he said with a warm chuckle. "Right after you finish that, how do you say, fantasy?"

"Yeah, Louie, it's only a fantasy, but it's a start, right?"

"Right! And will there be dragons?"

"No, I'm afraid there aren't any dragons."

"But there's lots of magic," Wallace Jackson said, coming up from behind and slapping me on the back. "The Rollin' Homeboy here let me scan some of it, Louie. It be *bad!*"

"I'm sure it is, Wallace," Louie said with a laugh. "You see to it that he stays with it until it's done. Right?"

"Affirmative!"

"Okay, okay," I said, brushing mozzarella crumbs out of my short beard. "What about lunch?"

"The usual," Wallace said seriously.

"You mean, whatever I'm buying?"

"Exactly!"

When Wallace and Tamara carried a tray full of selected slices toward their favorite table, I paid Louie and asked when we could talk.

"How's one-thirty?"

"One-thirty," I said, "will be just fine."

I found Lenny Gordon standing just outside the Bavarian House, sampling something that a young saleslady was frying up in an electric skillet. By the look on her face and the grease on his fingers, I suspected that not only had Lenny eaten more than his fair share of freebies but that the sight of his great bulk in the doorway wasn't helping the general passersby give in to their innate desire for greasy, cholesterol-laden food.

"Lenny," I said, "I need some expert advice. Got a minute?"

"Maybe," he said, looking at me with suspicion. "What do you want?"

"I want to buy you a soft drink. After that hot sausage, I bet you could use something cold, eh?"

"Yeah. Yeah I could."

We took a café-type table across the concourse by the cookie boutique, so I ended up paying for Lenny's jumbo chocolate chip number as well.

"I was wondering about something, Lenny," I said, trying not to watch the way he inhaled the oversized cookie. "You don't miss much around here; I mean, you've got a natural eye for crime and the like. Where would somebody get the kind of drug stash that killed Martha Galliger?"

"You should be asking those kids of yours," he said, his patented sneer returning to his fat face. "Yeah, I know you think I'm too tough on them, but you'd better wise up. A week before your wedding, I just missed catching the blond brat in a drug deal," Lenny went on, leaning over and lowering his voice, "and I've already identified his supplier down in the OPD mug files. If that pusher shows up here again, he's mine. And if I can take down your mall rats at the same time, so much the better."

"Okay, Lenny, I know you don't like the kids. They hassle you, they don't respect you, and, who knows, maybe they just remind you that you're not young anymore, but did you actually *see* Billy Simpson buying drugs from someone?"

"It don't work like that," he said, shoving the last of the cookie into his mouth. "The supplier drops the drugs somewhere—like in one of the big planters around the mall—then one of the mall rats comes by later to pick them up. After he sells the stuff to his buddies, he puts the money back in the same location."

"Isn't that kind of risky?"

"Would you rather lose your drug money or get caught passing the stuff and have your butt thrown in the can?"

Good point. "But you said you *almost* caught Bill?"

"That's right. First I saw him talking to a suspicious-looking punk who turned out to be Willis Dent, a pusher with a record as long as your arm. The OPD told me his street name is Snake, and that he's big in that new street gang, the Vipers. The cops also told me what to look for; and sure enough, the next time I saw old Snake, he strolled into the mall—smooth as you please—walked around a little, and then strolled back out."

"But you didn't actually see him drop any drugs?"

"Well, no, not exactly, but a half hour later your little friend comes along and starts digging around in the plants out in front of Jacob's Clothiers . . . and he wasn't hunting for Easter eggs either."

The look of satisfaction in Lenny's heavily lidded eyes made me uncomfortable. One big difference between Leonard Gordon and Billy Simpson—beyond a considerable disparity in size, of course—was guile. When Billy lied, it was both obvious and unpremeditated, a knee-jerk survival instinct that never really fooled anyone nor accomplished anything substantive. Guileful folks, however, are driven by ulterior motive, and they can mix the truth and the lie at will, creating whatever impression best suits their purpose.

A person with the gift of comforting, according to Pastor Bob McClarrin, can often tell if someone is lying just by watching their eyes. I don't think I have that particular gift, but it would have been interesting to test my theory about whether or not Emily Warner did by having her observe my conversation with Big Lenny.

"So that's when you saw Billy with drugs?"

The security chief hesitated, pondering how he would answer. That in itself said something—only I had no idea what that something was.

"No," Lenny said at last. "No, I didn't. And I'm not happy about admitting this, but he ditched them somehow before I could corner him. I'm, ah, not as fast as I used to be." He brushed cookie crumbs off his white uniform shirt and black clip-on neck tie. "But I'll nail him next time. You can take that to the bank."

Louie and I sat in the sunny window overlooking East Colonial Drive. The view was pleasant, but the atmosphere was polluted.

"You're going to kill yourself if you keep chain-smoking those things, Louie."

"So they tell me."

"And you're probably killing me too."

"Sorry about that." He snubbed a butt out against the heel of his shoe while exhaling smoke from the fresh one he had just lit. "Everybody's got to die sooner or later."

"I've heard that. By the way, did Agent Fredericks talk to you about our little theory?"

Louie's good humor evaporated. "I know he's your friend, Stick, and he's probably a nice enough guy, but you'll have to excuse me if I don't have much goodwill for the FBI."

I began to waver in my resolve to delve into Louie's territory . . . whatever that territory might be. He crushed out the nearly new cigarette without lighting another and stared out across the parking lot to the highway beyond.

"Why, Louie?" I held my breath.

"Because I am Sicilian!" he said, turning to stare at me with dark eyes I'd never really seen before. "Because I moved here from New York City!" He banged his left fist on the table between us and opened his hand slowly, palm up. "And, because I make pizza."

"Louie, look, I didn't know. . . ."

"You didn't know what? That I was mob?" Luigi Leone laughed, but there was no sign of mirth. "America. It is the land of freedom and opportunity . . . so long as you don't trigger a certain profile match in the government's great computerized mind." With his right forefinger, he began to write an imaginary list on his left palm. "Question: What was born on the island of Sicily, immigrated to the United States, grew up in the streets of New York's Little Italy, and then built a pizza-by-the-slice business with his own hands?"

I sat frozen. His intensity was far beyond anything I had expected. And I should have known better.

"The computer," he went on more steadily, "is programmed to give just one answer to that question—along with a footnote that such a person must be audited every year by the IRS. Just because." The light in Louie's eyes seemed to ignite as a new thought came to him suddenly. He used his finger to cross out the invisible words on his hand. "Here," he said, starting over. "What about this? What grew up in America, fell off a roof, broke his back, and then lived out his years in a wheelchair?"

The light began to dawn, and my breathing grew easier.

"How many people," Louie said with satisfaction as he watched my face, "know that there are other answers to that question besides 'cripple' and 'invalid'? Are you invalid, Stick Foster?"

Touché.

▽

10

I LEARNED SOMETHING about discrimination against Italian-Americans from Luigi, but when he unwound a little, I also learned that his life was not altogether as tidy as he might have liked. This last, as a matter of principle, he had not discussed with Agent Fredericks. But undoubtedly Stanley already knew.

"To open a shop like this," Louie explained, motioning with his arm toward the small pizzeria, "you need a lease. Leases are hard to come by, they're expensive, and they're often sold years before the ground on which the mall sits is ever broken.

"Occasionally, however, an older mall like this one decides to remodel and add a food court. *If* you have the necessary connections, that is, if you know someone who knows a broker who keeps up on this sort of thing, then you *might* get a chance to bid."

"Mm."

"Yes. But what if a guy comes up to you and says: 'Luigi Leone, I understand you are in the market for a mall food shop lease. Would such a lease in Orlando, Florida, be of interest to you?' "

"And someone said this to you?"

"Worse," Louie said with a wry chuckle. "He went on to say that I wouldn't have to bid against anyone; he knew the lawyer handling the leases; I could walk to the guy's office from my Little Italy storefront shop."

"Sounds too good to be true."

"That's what I thought until I went to the lawyer and found out what it would cost me. I've often wondered whether an auction would have been cheaper."

"So you got the lease."

"Yes," Louie said, waving his arm again. "You see my kingdom before you."

"Did you break any laws?"

"No."

"Did the broker break any laws?"

"No."

"Did the lawyer break any laws?"

"No."

"So what's the problem?"

"Well it seems the lawyer had, somewhere in his past, represented someone who *was* in the mob."

"Did you know?"

"No. But should it have mattered if I had?"

"So that's all?"

"That's enough. Ask your friend. I've been under investigation by the FBI, the IRS, the DEA, you name it, ever since."

"I'm sorry, Louie."

"Yeah, me too."

"Can you think of any reason why anyone, mob or otherwise, might want you out of the way?"

"None."

Mm.

It all happened very fast. I left Louie, rolled down to the rest rooms by the mall offices, and pushed around the heavy door. The scruffy, black-haired young man in a leather vest and tattered jeans backed quickly out of one of the stalls and looked purposefully at the door that had just closed behind me. I didn't notice his face; it was the serpentine tattoo on his right forearm and the knife in his right hand that drew my full attention.

"Bad timing, crip," he said, striding at me, the shiny blade level with my face.

I was bracing for the attack when Billy Simpson lunged out of the toilet stall with a scream and hit the approaching hoodlum from behind. They fell across the footrests of my chair, and as I blocked the wildly swinging blade, we all toppled toward the sinks. The young man's knife hand struck porcelain and the weapon clattered harmlessly across the floor tiles. Billy, still clinging to the guy's back with one hand, flicked his switchblade and was preparing to bury it to the hilt. I caught his wrist just in time, giving Snake the chance to scramble past my overturned wheelchair and through the door.

"Lemme go! I'll kill him!" Billy Simpson squirmed in my grip. His face was bleeding, and I wasn't about to let him run off through the mall waving a knife.

"Bill, enough! It's over. Now put that thing away before Big Lenny shows up. Here, help me back into my wheelchair."

That seemed to get his attention, though the adrenaline-enhanced anger was slow to subside and his hands shook. He set my old folder upright, locked the brakes, and held it while I transferred from the floor to the chair. Then he noticed his face in the wall-long mirror. He was white as the proverbial sheet by the time I finished making a cold wet-pack with several brown paper towels.

"Here," I said, "hold this on the cut and follow me out to my car . . . casually, like nothing happened. Can you do that?"

He nodded slowly.

"Good." I wrapped Snake's knife in a dry paper towel and stuck it next to my laptop computer in the black canvas pack that hung on the back of my wheelchair. "Let's go."

As we sped north and west toward Florida Hospital, I used the car phone to call ahead.

"Joe O'Donnel."

"Hi, Doc. Stick Foster. Can you meet me in the ER in about three or four minutes?"

"I don't do ER anymore, Nick. You know that."

"For old time's sake?"

"What old time's sake? You were a pain in the butt."

"It's important."

"That's what they all say. See you down there."

Joe O'Donnel is a doctor of internal medicine—a good one. He was my primary physician from the day I broke my back until the day a Florida state rehab nurse referred me to Craig Spinal Rehabilitation Hospital in Denver. Joe took that kind of personally.

"This is good," he said when we were as alone as the white curtained partitions allowed. He put a firm hand on Billy Simpson's shoulder and took a closer look at the thin red laceration along the boy's left jawline. "I hope you're his guardian?"

"No, but I called his mother. She's on her way."

"I can't—"

"I know, Doc. Look. How about you sew him up real neat, now, and when his mom gets here and wants you to take the stitches out, I'll pay you overtime."

"Who cut you, son?" Joe asked as he cleaned up the surgically tidy wound.

"I, ah . . ."

"He fell over my wheelchair," I said. "We got tangled up over in the Palmetto Plaza public rest room. I kind of take up more than my share of room."

"Right, Nick. And there just happened to be a scalpel lying around too. Lies just aren't your thing, so give me a break."

After injecting a local anesthetic, Joe sutured up the wound so neatly it was obvious that the scar, at least, would not be too bad. "I don't think he'll need any putty work—not there. It's good you didn't get cut up here, son," he said, running his finger higher up along Bill's cheek. "Bad scar then. Did you get in a lick at the other guy?"

"Please, Joe," I interrupted. "Let it go, okay? It's important."

"There you go again. I hope that phrase is in your writer's dictionary of clichés, because it's certainly in mine."

Billy Simpson's mom was a piece of work. I had only spoken to her on the phone twice, but knew she was the nervous Nellie type. I hadn't looked forward to meeting her at all, let alone in a hospital emergency department. She swept into the curtain-walled room like a butterfly with tattered wings.

"Billy! What have you done? Are you in trouble again? I'm so sorry, Doctor . . . I just don't know what to do with him. The boy's father left us, you see, and I try to do my best, but—"

"Mrs. Simpson," I said. "It's all right. Bill isn't in trouble. We just had a little collision."

"I don't have any insurance," she said to Dr. O'Donnel as he placed a gauze bandage on Bill's left cheek. "So I don't know—"

"Not to worry, Mrs. Simpson," Joe said with a broad smile. "Mr. Foster is taking care of this. I need to see you in a week, Bill, and we'll take those stitches out. Okay?"

"Okay," the boy said. "Thanks."

Bill looked reproachfully at his mother as she stood there wringing her hands. Her light hair was unkempt, her clothing worn and dirty, and her makeup nonexistent. She was a woman in her thirties who might have been pretty, I suppose, but she looked worn enough to be twice her age—a testament to Neanderthal men and helpless women everywhere. I knew the statistics but hoped against all odds that the sins of the father would not visit the son.

"Can we go now?" is what Billy said to me.

"Thank you, Mr. Foster," his mother said, "for taking an interest in Billy. He needs a man to—"

"It's all right," I said. "Bill's my friend, that's all."

Mrs. Simpson looked confused as a nurse handed her a clipboard and asked her to sign the form that would give Joe legal permission to do what he had already done. Bill stood up a little straighter and we walked out to the cashier's window together.

"Well, bud," I said when both his mother and the good doctor were gone and we sat waiting for our bill to be totaled, "I think you and I have to have a *real* talk."

▽

11

BILL FOLLOWED ME through the hospital corridors, obviously ill at ease. I deliberately took him through the physical and occupational therapy departments where I'd spent so many hours learning how not to walk. I exchanged greetings with the therapists who remembered me and tried to encourage a few struggling patients for whom the hard road back was just beginning. Then I took him out a little-used door on that wing's east wall. The well-tended lawn stretched out away from us and then downhill to a small blue-green lake. The concrete pad by the door was just big enough for both of us and I motioned for Billy to sit down.

"I used to sneak out here and hide," I said, locking my wheelchair brakes and tipping back against the shady wall. "The hospital always felt so cold, and in the mornings this wall is warm and bright; it just seemed to put life back into me somehow."

"You ever get caught?"

"Yeah, I got caught. But the therapist who caught me was sneaking out here for the same reason. It was our little secret from then on. You and I need to start sharing some secrets too, bud."

"How come you don't call me Bart?"

The question came out of left field, but it was a start. "Do you like being compared to a half-witted punk cartoon character just because your last name is the same?"

"Well, no, I guess not."

"Good. I wouldn't like it either."

He thought that through for a bit. "And why do you keep telling people I'm your friend, Stick? I mean, I'm still just a kid."

"Let me get this straight. You're saying we can't be friends because I'm too old?"

"Jeez, no. I didn't mean that."

"I hope not. Is it because I'm in a wheelchair?" I asked as seriously as I could. It wasn't easy not to smile.

"No! Come on, Stick, it's nothing like that. It's just that . . . It's just that grown-ups never like me."

"Mm. So what you're really trying to say is that I'm not very good at being an adult. I can live with that if you can."

"Man, you're weird." He was finally smiling, even though the stitches must have made it difficult. And even with the white gauze bandage on his jaw, the smile made his face look healthy and whole. Every kid needs to smile sometimes. Just like adults.

"It's like this, Bill. I'm a Potential junkie. Potential isn't what things are; it's what they can be . . . if we hang tough. So I get ahead of myself a lot. I think maybe some other adults might only see Billy Simpson, the kid who doesn't know who he is yet and tells everybody a different story about it. Or Billy Simpson, the mall rat with an attitude." I snatched the black Motley Crue hat off his platinum mop and put it on, cocked wickedly to one side. I sneered and shook my head like I was totally too cool. Then I threw it back at him and locked my fingers behind my head.

"I guess I see Billy Simpson, the grown-up who survived being a teenager and remembers when Stick Foster was his friend. I really just want to be sure there's someone around who'll sneak pizza to me in the old people's home."

He laughed for a few seconds, but then the old clouds came back across his face. "You know when I'm lying, don't you?"

"Yes. Usually."

"And you still like me?"

"Yeah, and so do your other friends."

"You mean they . . ."

It was my turn to laugh. The semi-innocence of youth getting a peek at the cold, hard realities of life . . . even the best TV sitcoms never quite get the look of it right.

"They all accept me even though I can't walk, don't they, Bill?" He nodded. "And they accept you even though you're so full of crap, half the flies in Wisconsin are getting on tour buses to come down here and see you for themselves."

His eyes widened, alarm stirring slightly, but he just couldn't resist my grinning stare. In the end, he sheepishly nodded assent, tumbled off the concrete stoop and out into the sunshine a dozen yards away, and lay there stretched out in the plush green grass.

"Feels kinda good, doesn't it?"

"Yeah," he said, "it does."

So we talked. We talked more than we ever had, but Billy was either lying to me again, or he was just so ill at ease with the truth, it sounded the same. He swore that he wasn't doing drugs, but that when Snake had approached him, flaunting a fat roll of not-so-legal tender, he just couldn't resist the chance to make some big bucks.

It was, like much of Billy Simpson's young life, a venture bound for disaster.

"He told me where to pick up the stuff, who to deliver it to, and when to drop his money back in the same place. Easy."

But, according to Billy, he arrived at the planter outside Jacob's at just the right time, only to find that there was nothing there. Worse than that, Big Lenny was bearing down on him, calling for back-up on his walkie-talkie. As unpleasant as his capture and interrogation by the Palmetto Plaza security police might have been, he soon had Snake after him as well, to the tune of $500 in lost revenues. Or at least so he said.

And I really wanted to believe him too. But there were so many unanswered questions. *If* Willis Dent put a drug delivery in that planter—and his attack on Billy suggested that he might have—who besides Bill would know to retrieve it? Leonard Gordon was one possibility, but why wouldn't he just wait and catch the young mall rat with the goods? Big Lenny would certainly have enjoyed sending him off to the Orange County Juvenile Detention Center.

Fred Lucas came to mind. He spent a good deal of his time watching the pedestrian traffic on the mall concourse outside Jacob's. For that matter, it could have been Ernest Boyle, or any other mall employee, or any shopper as well. Or Billy Simpson.

Getting those same drugs from the planter to my wedding and into a red-and-white paper cup of punch was a stretch, but it was the only route available at the time, so I went with it.

Billy and I talked until the shadow of the hospital's east wing stretched all the way down the lawn, across Lake Estelle, and out onto Mills Avenue. On the drive home, I tried to focus on the most present danger.

"What are you going to do about Snake and his gang?"

"I don't know. Stay out of their way, I guess."

We needed legal help. I picked up the car phone and called the law office of the Three R's. After a brief discussion with my live-in barrister, I translated for Billy.

"You've got two choices that you can choose between or combine," I said. "The first is to go to the police. We've got Snake's knife, with his prints and your blood on it. I didn't actually see him cut you, but considering what I did see, nobody's going to believe he was just giving you a shave. Of course, that means telling the police about your little business arrangement."

Billy's eyes got big, and he was shaking his head from side to side with some enthusiasm.

"It's not that bad. Sam says that if you never actually handled or sold any of his drugs, you're safe. There's no law against *thinking* about committing a crime." The boy's head never stopped its negative movements.

"The other option is something called a restraining order. We go before a judge, present our evidence that Mr. Dent threatened your person, and request that the court issue a restraining order against him. It's only temporary, but if, while it's in force, Willis comes within, say, five hundred feet of you, the police can just lock him up for disobeying the judge."

"Let's do that one," Billy said without hesitation.

"I thought you might say that, but a court order won't help you if Snake, or one of the other Vipers, gets to you before you can get the police on him," I said soberly. "I think we should go to the police as well."

"No way."

"Okay, you're the boss."

▽

12

"SO YOU AND your adopted son have a piece of paper," Sam said between spoonfuls of minestrone. "You and I both know that doesn't mean anything to a drug gang. What are you going to do next?"

The supper crowd at Angelo's was light, but the traffic outside on Semoran Boulevard was brisk. "I'm not sure. I think I'll ask Ben to let me do a piece on the Vipers; you know, a 'Gangs Move Uptown' kind of thing."

Sam rolled her eyes as she chewed her garlic bread; she didn't need to say anything. Ben Dawson was a pretty good city editor, but that's not why he kept that job at the *Orlando Sentinel*. He was a bona fide, make-nice public relations bloodhound. If there was a way to make Orlando look any better than it already looked; if there was a way to draw new attractions, businesses, and tourists; if there was a way to move heaven and earth to put a happy face on the local scene, Benjamin "Good News" Dawson would ferret it out and put it in print. It was only a matter of time, insiders agreed, before the jovial newspaper man ran for mayor . . . and won.

"Okay," I said, savoring my manicotti, "so it won't be easy. But Ben's not the only guy who can make a sow's ear look like a silk purse. Maybe I'll just slip a couple of Viper interviews in with my mall report."

The storm that blew into Sam's gaze came out of nowhere. One minute it was fair skies and warm temperatures; a second later, there were hurricane warning flags up along the coast and frost warnings in the orange groves. I wasn't sure *what* I'd done, but I knew just enough to know that I had, indeed, done *something*. I suddenly wanted to ask the waiter if he'd mind turning off the air-conditioning.

"What?" I knew it was the wrong question the instant I asked it.

Sam took her time. She placed her soup spoon neatly beside the milky white bowl, wiped her mouth demurely with the red linen napkin, and then gently shook off the remaining crumbs before returning the cloth to her lap. For reasons that escaped me at the time, the experience was reminiscent of looking down the barrel of a kidnapper's .45-caliber Colt automatic. But that was a different disaster.

"Writing about the Vipers is one thing," Sam said, too calmly. "Interviewing them is out of the question; especially if you're the only witness when one of them carved up a minor with his knife."

Up north, they call it wind chill. The thermometer might say it's a balmy 38 degrees Fahrenheit, but it *feels* like ten below zero. Outside, Altamonte Springs was experiencing a rather warm summer night; but inside Angelo's Italian restaurant, there was drifting snow.

Then I made another mistake. A big one. The words came unbidden to my lips, a personal jest never intended for the light of day.

"Yes, dear."

The restaurant went dead still. The only noise was the sound of Sam's wheelchair bumping the front door on its way out. By the time I paid the bill and rushed after her, Sam's red Mustang convertible was gone, lost in the busy traffic.

It was just a joke.

Okay, it was a sarcastic and insensitive joke. My dad gave me lots of advice before he died; nuggets of wisdom about money, friends, politics, religion, and comfortable shoes. It came to me suddenly—sitting there in Angelo's parking lot—that I couldn't remember his ever having passed on any tips about marriage.

The sun was shining—it was 82 degrees at ten o'clock the next morning—but my window seat at the Palmetto Plaza Mall food court didn't feel nearly as warm as usual; I was learning that thawing out is hard to do. Sleeping with Sam Wagner-Foster had been the warmest, most wonderful experience of my harried journey on the planet. I wondered how something so life affirming could turn so lethal so fast.

"Like, who died anyway?"

A soft hand ran across my shoulder before Emily Warner took the seat across the table and aimed her disconcerting brown-eyed gaze directly at me. The morning sun streamed in the big plate-glass window and lit up her Day-Glo nylon jacket like the laser light show at a rock concert. Her sunglasses rested on top of her head, the electric lime green legs showing through her short jet black hair in several places.

"Hi, Emily. You're out and about early today. What's up?"

"Not you. Like, what's so bogus?"

"Nothing," I said, waving my hand and putting on one of my best smiles. Emily didn't notice; she was coming straight into my head through my eyes.

"I think, *not,*" she said firmly. "You're a worse liar than the Bart Man, Stick. Whatever it is," she added, reaching across the table and placing both her hands on top of mine, "I'm sorry."

If empathy has a face, it must look just like Emily Warner's. Pastor Bob said comforters care right from the heart; they just can't help it.

"Anyway, I wanted to talk to you about Bart," she went on. I started feeling awkward about the hand holding and withdrew as casually as I could, reaching for my backpack and retrieving my computer as a cover for my discomfort. "Did you know that he, like, lives here?"

"Sure. I've dropped him off at his house."

"No," Emily said, shaking her head and gesturing with her arm, "*here.*"

"*Here?* The mall, *here?* What do you mean, Emily?"

"I mean, like, he sleeps here at night . . . at least some of the time."

"Where? One of the stores? How do you know?"

Emily laughed at my astonishment but shrugged her shoulders. "We don't know where, but probably not in a store. Those all have megasecurity gates. But, like, Bart just sort of stays behind a lot when the rest of us leave. We used to think he liked to stay as late as possible—you know, until Big Lenny has to kick him out—but Danny, Jeremy, and I waited around a couple of times. Bart just never came out."

"He probably left by another door, that's all."

"I think, *not.*"

Mm.

The mall rats filtered in over the next two hours, all of them knowing that I was a soft touch and would spring for lunch. Billy Simpson arrived last. His bandage was gone, and the delicate black stitches that ran down the line of his jaw brought immediate attention from his friends.

"Yo, Bart," Wallace Jackson said enthusiastically, "that's a proper scratch. He cut you pretty good, huh?"

"Does it, like, hurt?" Emily asked, running her fingers gently along Billy's face.

"There is a relatively low concentration of surface sensory nerve endings in that part of the face," Jeremy Palmer announced. He leaned over to inspect Billy's laceration more closely. "The muscles controlling the mandible are here and here, and there are various glands, including those producing saliva, just underneath here."

Billy swatted away Jeremy's hand. "Thanks for sharing, Geek," he said. "Next time use a chalkboard."

"I'll get the drinks," Tamara said, hopping up, obviously anxious to contribute something positive to the moment.

As we ate Louie's pizza, it occurred to me that something was wrong about the mall. The crowd was average, the noise level in the food court was like that of any other day, but something was different. Whatever it was, I felt certain it would come to me eventually. In the meantime, I had another proposition for my mall rats.

"It's like a posse!" Danny Singer said when I had passed out personal beepers from the Southeast Electronics store and outlined my idea about looking out for Billy and tracking down Snake for "questioning."

"I don't know about this," Jeremy said, studying the small gadget before clipping it on his belt. "These matters are sometimes better left to the proper authorities. One of us could get hurt."

"One of us has already been hurt," Emily said, swatting Jeremy with the back of one hand and pointing at Billy with the other.

"Oh, yes, well, sorry," Jeremy said. "I just meant—"

"We know what you meant," Wallace said with a laugh. "Don't worry, Tamara will protect you!"

I don't know exactly why I paired them up the way I did; maybe I was experimenting with their "gifts." And I didn't really think talking to Snake would lead me to Martha Galliger's killer, but it was all I had. Tamara and Jeremy, Danny and Wallace, and Billy and Emily. It wasn't a very logical military or tactical deployment, but since my object was to gather information and avoid combat, it felt right somehow.

Tamara threw herself in front of Jeremy, lashing out at invisible attackers with her hands and feet, saying "hi!" and "ha!" and making high-pitched whining sounds just like those in the late-night karate movies. Jeremy's ears turned red as he tried to wave her away; to his credit, the precocious youngster knew a good jest when he saw one, and he laughed right along with the others. The others, that is, with the exception of Billy Simpson. He didn't seem to appreciate my efforts on his behalf.

"Does everybody understand what to do?" I asked when they settled down. I showed them the mug shot of Snake again. "Don't talk to him. Don't try to stop him by yourself. Let's hear the routine again."

They loved this part of my plan. I can't say that I liked more than a few of the rap artists who seemed to be playing on nearly every youngster's radio, but if you want a kid to memorize something in a hurry, there's probably no better way to do it than to give it a rap beat. Only Billy wanted no part of it. While the others looked at their crib notes one last time and Wallace pursed his lips and started the beat-box intro he had created for the occasion, Billy Simpson backed away from the table.

Don't want no hassle; don't want no jive.
Just lookin' for the Snake; gonna take 'im alive.
If he heads for the front doors, beep one times.
It be two for Sears and three for Burdines.

The mall rats didn't whisper this time; they were really getting into it. While Wallace performed his controlled-spitting beat-box solo between verses, Tamara and Emily stood up side by side and started a synchronized dance routine, which Danny and Jeremy both jumped up to join. The lunch crowd had all stopped to watch, for good reason. The kids were great.

Four for the north door, five for the west,
East is six, 'cause we like that best.
We're the Palmetto Seven, and we run this ranch.
And seven is the number for Maison Blanche.

I'm not exactly sure how it turned into a rap version of a conga line, but before I knew it, I was being pushed around the food court, followed by a growing train of dancing rappers. First the cleanup crews joined in. Charlie Martin's wonderful smile grew even bigger as he bopped into the line pushing his rolling trash receptacle and throwing his head from side to side with the beat. Within moments, what seemed like half the food court employees and customers had picked up on the easy words and were parading around behind us. I'm sure no one else had a clue what the song meant, but that didn't seem to stand in their way.

Louie stood laughing behind his pizza counter and clapped his hands when I looked up helplessly and shrugged on my way past. By the forth or fifth time through the routine—with frequent solo performances from various participants—everyone in the mall's north end must have come to watch. The crowd, still hastening up the escalator, forced its way in and around the balcony railing, loudly cheering the impromptu entertainment, so it took longer than it might have otherwise for them to realize that a shot had been fired somewhere in the courtyard area below them.

▽

13

THE COURTYARD IS one of those indoor scenic areas high-dollar architects dream about: two stories of open space, framed in glass and towering royal palms. The fountain, the stage, and the see-through elevator all give it a movie-location look that rivals anything any larger mall might have to offer. The maintenance crews must be on special notice about the courtyard, because—like Main Street at Disney World—litter barely hits the ground before some worker with a broom and a long-handled, swivel-bucketed dustpan whisks it away.

When I made my way through the stunned crowd at the balcony, I looked down to see one of those diligent litter luggers standing in shocked silence over the crumpled hulk of the mall's security chief, Leonard Gordon. Even from that distance, I could see the growing crimson stain on the front of his white uniform shirt. There was usually a MedVac Rescue Unit across the highway to the south, but something told me that even if Big Lenny had fallen directly into an ambulance with that chest wound (it was already producing a small lake on the mall floor below us), it wouldn't have made any difference.

I realized, as well, what had seemed odd about my morning at the mall: I hadn't seen Leonard Gordon once. He usually strolled by several times an hour, regardless of where

I might be parked in the sprawling concourse. From 9:30 A.M., when I arrived, until the shooting, moments before 1:00 P.M., the security chief had not passed through the food court. Big Lenny—pussyfoot or not—is hard to miss.

I felt a familiar hand on my shoulder. "Where's Bart?" Emily whispered in my ear. "Jeremy says he and Big Lenny had, like, a bad fight last night before the mall closed."

Mm. Two fights for him in two days. Maybe it was the moon.

"I don't know," I answered. "Let's split up and look for him. Tell the others: use the teams, same signals, meet back here in an hour, and how 'bout you come with me?"

"Sure. Be right back."

We drove ten blocks south to the Simpson's dilapidated white rental house, where Emily talked briefly to Billy's mother before returning to my car.

"I just said, like, we were looking for him," she reassured me. "Nothing about the shooting or anything."

"Good. Well?"

"She hasn't seen him since the hospital."

"I dropped him off here at dinnertime," I said, thinking more seriously about Emily's suggestion that Billy might be living at the mall.

"I told you," she said softly.

Another thought struck me at that moment—a bad thought. I pointed to the car phone and had Emily dial Stanley Frederick's office at the federal building.

"Hi, Stick. What's up?"

"Stan, there's just been a shooting at the Palmetto Plaza Mall. Lenny Gordon, you know, the big security guy?"

"You mean Pussyfoot?"

"You know his nickname?"

"Sure. He's a frustrated investigator. Never made it as a real cop but always tried to be a part of something ongoing or instigate some new investigation. You know the type. Likes to be thought of as one of the boys—even though he's not. Old Pussyfoot just loved to talk the talk, though. He'd call the OPD, or us, several times a week and fill us in on some new crime theory he had. Always had some angle. Is he still alive?"

"I don't know, but I doubt it. MRU was arriving when I left, but I'd be really surprised if he made it to the hospital. How did you know about his nickname?"

"Well, he fits a certain profile," Stanley said. "Once in a while, one of those never-made-it-as-a-real-cop types gets frustrated at the law enforcement community that didn't welcome them with open arms and, well, sort of switches sides. Also, most of them are, or were at one time, rent-a-cops."

"Mm. So you investigated Lenny?"

"SOP."

"It makes sense to me, I guess, but I think you'd better run down whatever's left of Lenny now and find out what hit him. I've got a bad feeling about it."

"Why?"

"What kind of loads do you guys use, Stan?"

"Glasier safety slugs, so?"

"Lots of internal damage, drop a bull elephant without coming out the other side?"

"Something like that."

"Well, Big Lenny was down like a ton of loose bricks, he was bleeding like all of his insides were torn up, and . . . your gun's never turned up, has it?"

"Oh great."

The soft, anguished sigh came from deep inside him, carrying across the cellular telephone connection like an invisible heartbreak. I just waited.

"What about your mall rats?" Stanley said after a few seconds of uncomfortable silence.

"All present and accounted for," I answered, swallowing hard, "except for one."

"The Simpson boy, right?"

"That's right. We're looking for him now."

Emily and I cruised the mall parking lot several times, looking for Billy in every shadow. By the time we parked and went inside, the ambulance was long gone, but Orlando

Police Department representatives had detained a large number of shoppers and were questioning them one at a time. The courtyard was spotless and, while the police had inspected and taken pictures of the crime scene, the gruesome cleanup (when permission was finally given to carry it out) was probably accomplished in seconds.

Emily and I took the glass elevator up to the food court and settled back in at our table where—even in the midst of chaos—Charlie Martin had cheerfully cleaned up the mess we had left behind. Danny and Wallace, then Tamara and Jeremy joined us moments later. They had all been questioned, but Louie had come forward immediately to vouch that they had been entertaining the lunch crowd at the time of the shooting.

"He ain't here," Danny announced. "No way, no how."

"We searched *every* store," Wallace added.

"Us too," Tamara said.

"He's here." There was no question in Jeremy Palmer's voice. "Bart has a secret place where he hides until the mall closes. I just know he does. All we have to do is figure out where it is."

"Look, guys," I said, "I'm gonna ask you about something that you've been asked about before. This time, however, if you're not straight with me, you could be accessories to a murder."

Their eyes opened a little wider, but nobody looked away.

"Do any of you know anything—anything at all—about Agent Fredericks's missing gun?"

Five heads moved solemnly from side to side, and I'd have bet almost anything that they were all telling me the truth. For their sakes, I prayed that they were.

I sent them to search one more time and told them to find Ernest Boyle and ask him to please come up as soon as he had a chance. While they were gone, I interviewed several cops, shoppers, and dustpan operators before typing up a story on my laptop computer. Louie let me plug in to his telephone line long enough to dump the piece on Ben Dawson's desk. Good News Dawson wasn't going to like it at all, and while it would have been front page news in any other city in the country, my guess was that it would be hidden, as innocuously as possible, on page two. National and international bad news are okay on page one, occasionally, but Orange County bad news just isn't printed there.

Television was something else again. By the time Ernest Boyle arrived, there were several camera crews reporting live from the crime scene, informing central Florida viewers that, in the midst of the crowded Palmetto Plaza Mall lunch hour, an unknown assailant had shot Leonard Gordon at point-blank range. As I watched them from the second-floor balcony, I learned that Big Lenny had been pronounced dead on arrival at Florida Hospital. Ballistic tests, according to one preppy-looking remote broadcaster, were being run, but the police had already confirmed reports that the mortal wound had, more than likely, been inflicted by a large-caliber handgun. And no one had seen a thing.

"What can I do for you, Nick Foster?"

"Hi, Ernest. I need an expert . . . a Palmetto Plaza Mall expert."

"Oh, well, I know some about the place, so to speak, but I'm not what you'd call an expert."

"You're just the man I need, Ernest. Don't be so modest."

When I explained the kids' suspicions about Billy Simpson staying in the mall throughout the night, a wry smile crept across the head maintenance man's narrow face.

"I knew it!" he said when I paused. "I keep finding signs—little things really—so the notion has crossed my mind, so to speak, that somebody besides the night security patrol has been in here. You want me to help you catch him?" Ernest asked with an adventurous smile.

"That's exactly what I want, Ernest. I knew you were my man."

We worked out a place to meet, I promised to be there at 10:00 P.M., and Ernest went back to work. The kids returned with nothing new to report, but Jeremy had begun formulating theories about how one might get into the mall's duct-work system. I listened with interest, certain that Ernest Boyle would know right away whether such a feat were possible.

Then I called home.

▽

14

"I'M SORRY."

We both said it at once, the sweetest words I'd ever heard. Marriages failing in the first few weeks are a Hollywood phenomenon; it just couldn't happen to us.

"I was scared, and then angry," Sam said, the tone of her voice suggesting that I should head home posthaste. I put the old Monte SS in gear and pointed it toward Goldenrod.

"And I had no business smarting off," I said. "It was a thoughtless joke. I love you more than you will ever imagine."

"Come home. Now."

No sooner said . . .

Sam wasn't thrilled about my returning to the mall that night, but nearly four hours of making up took the edge off her objections. As evidenced by the ball of brown fur curling up behind her knees, Sam was out for the count anyway. Butkis was seldom wrong. It wasn't easy for me to dress and climb back into my wheelchair, but Billy Simpson had a hold on me that I could neither explain nor dismiss.

I parked in one of the mall's handicapped spots, just outside the west entrance. The secluded lot was empty—no sign of Ernest Boyle—but I was early. Retrieving a scratch pad from the dash and blowing off the dust, I looked again at my suspect list for Martha Galliger's murder. I started to cross off Leonard Gordon but realized, even as I pressed my felt-tip pen to the page, that his being murdered didn't rule him out as a suspect in the earlier homicide. I also wanted to scratch off all the mall rats—with the exception of Billy Simpson—but that was just wishful thinking.

I created a column on the right side of the page, heading it "Big Lenny." I made check marks across from the names listed to the left, but only if it were *possible*—to the best of my knowledge—that they might have wandered into the mall that morning and committed a walk-by shooting. I could almost picture someone strolling along with a handgun hidden under a newspaper or a windbreaker. That thought gave me an addition to the list.

They called themselves the Strollers Club, and they had their own T-shirts and fanny packs. They even held club meetings. There was an official course and accompanying workout regime that had been mapped out by the project's cosponsor, the Orlando Regional Medical Center. Stroller members even got special deals from participating mall merchants.

I'd interviewed several Strollers for my continuing feature, and now remembered seeing two or three of them at my wedding. I had a theory about how to guess the severity of their individual health scares (i.e., strokes, arthritis, excessive weight) that hinged on how stringently they adhered to the course, and especially on how precisely they marched into every alcove and corner en route, as if rounding off a corner might send them straight to the emergency room. But that's another story.

It felt good not to be able to check five of my six mall rats. Charlie Martin, the special food court cleanup man, was out of the question, even if he hadn't been with us. Louie was clapping his hands and singing along with the rest of us when the shot went off. I suppose he could have "arranged" something; the Feds might think so. There was that stereotyping he'd warned me about.

Ernest was an unlikely suspect, but I had no solid reason to dismiss him. The same was true of Fred Lucas, the pipe-smoking senior salesman at Jacob's Clothiers, as well as a hundred other salespeople throughout the mall. It would be time consuming, but relatively simple, to determine whether they were on the sales floor at the time of the shooting. I concluded my check marking with a reluctant mark across from "All members—R.P. Church" and "All members—Orlando Orange Wheels."

"That really narrows it down," I said ruefully to my steering wheel. "From here on, solving these murders should be a piece of cake."

The afterglow of lovemaking had disappeared, and a cool northerly night breeze was giving me the chills. Rolling up the Monte's electric windows and accidentally hitting the power lock button was, perhaps, the most fortuitous thing I'd done in years. Before I could unlock the doors, shadowy figures came out of nowhere and surrounded my car. It didn't take a genius to figure out that the cobra being spray painted on my windshield meant that I was being honored with a visit from the Vipers.

Several things happened nearly at once, none of them good. As I reached instinctively for the ignition, three tires went flat and someone with a crowbar popped open my hood and yanked out the Monte's coil wire. The fourth tire died as I reached for the car phone, and "Snake" appeared outside the driver's-side window, slapping my short, black, cellular telephone antenna against his palm like a riding crop. Some perverse internal calculator told me there were five of them.

"We were looking for your little friend."

Snake's muffled voice was smug, spiteful. He leaned over and grinned at me through the glass. There are times when I miss my once whole and athletic body more than I do at other times. This was one of those times.

"But you'll do okay for now, crip."

The crowbar came through the passenger-side window, spraying rock candy–shaped pebbles of glass all over me. Looking in that direction, I saw more grins . . . and several bladed weapons. One young man nonchalantly opened and closed a long silver butterfly knife with practiced flips of his wrist and graceful movements of the fingers on his right hand.

Fear, anger, and helplessness make for a most unpleasant combination. My grip shifted and tightened around the felt-tip pen. When Edward Bulwer-Lytton wrote Act II of *Richelieu,* claiming that the pen was mightier than the sword, I'm fairly certain he wasn't facing the Vipers.

But I had a tire iron. And a bicycle pump, a white windbreaker, and a collapsible spin-fishing rig . . . all in the trunk. In the front seat, at my disposal, I had the pen. That, and a worthless car phone. And—if given time to gather them—a fuzzy collection of fumbled french fries. Snake was still grinning when the crowbar took out my back window and someone pulled my folded wheelchair out through the opening.

It was probably as futile as fighting off the Vipers with my pen, but the novelty of the thought-come-lately appealed to my growing sense of desperation. I moved my right hand to my belt slowly, hoping to avoid Snake's attention, and pressed my thumb five times against the beeper attached to my belt.

"Hey! What you got there?" shouted the butterfly knife. "He's got something on his belt," he said to Snake as he reached in the broken window and unlocked the passenger door before throwing it open and advancing, blade first.

"Leave him be!" Snake's voice was clearer now that two of my windows were gone, but the smugness was missing.

I looked back to my left and saw that a .45-caliber army automatic rested, business end first, against the young hoodlum's left temple. Ernest Boyle's other hand was full of long wavy hair, and he was busy whispering in Snake's right ear. The mall's scrawny fix-it man looked decidedly more threatening than I could ever have imagined.

"Everybody over here. Now!" Snake said, obviously following Ernest's orders. "Bring the wheelchair and put it by the door . . . knives on the ground . . . there. Sit down . . . back to back . . . there. Fast!"

"Glad to see you," I said to Ernest as I climbed unsteadily into my chair and looked at my Monte from the outside. "Look what they did to my car. Can we just kill 'em, Ernest, and stash their bodies under the mall somewhere?"

"No problem," Ernest said, glancing back at me with a

wink. "There's lots of little out-of-the-way-places, so to speak, in the bowels of that old mall where this scum could rot in peace, forever."

"Look," said Snake earnestly, "we've got money! We'll pay for your car . . . and more. We'll get you a new one . . . two!"

Police sirens approached from the west.

"You trash my car, threaten my person, and then offer me drug money and stolen vehicles. Am I getting this right? Almost be fun to see what the court does to repeat offenders who attack poor, defenseless crippled people," I said to Ernest.

"I did a story on prisons once. Did you know that even the coldest murderers on death row hate anybody who attacks a handicapped person? Most guys convicted of mugging somebody in a wheelchair die in prison, killed by their fellow prisoners—it's some kind of honor-code thing. I felt safer down at the Belle Glade correctional facility than I do here at the mall."

This was obviously a new concept to the Vipers, and I liked the effect it was having on them.

Emily Warner—bless her heart—had summoned the OPD to the west mall entrance when her beeper went off five times. By the time the police had sorted things out, checked the registration on Ernest's pistol, made out their preliminary report, and hauled off the Vipers, she had phoned all the mall rats who lived out of beeper range and rushed to meet them at Site 5. They stood around my Monte in reverent silence as the truck from an all-night towing service gently winched it up onto the shiny metal flatbed.

"As long as you're all here anyway," I said, as the truck and my car disappeared across the lot, "and if my hero, Mr. Boyle, doesn't mind, you might as well help us look for Billy."

"How 'bout it, Soda Speak!" Danny said, slapping the wiry maintenance man on the shoulder. "Can we come?"

"We can fit into much smaller spaces than you or Stick," Jeremy pointed out.

"And Bart might come out better for us," Emily added.

"Sure," Ernest said, taking his new hero status in stride. "The more the merrier . . . so to speak."

▽

15

I'VE ALWAYS WONDERED what Disney World would be like after everyone went home for the night, but I never thought much about a shopping mall in that way before. The first thing I noticed when Ernest unlocked the main entrance door and let us in was the quiet. A pervasive stillness lay on the sprawling concourse, disturbed only by the shuffling of our search party. The mausoleumlike feeling had an effect even on the usually exuberant mall rats. They stood clumped inside the doorway, staring uncertainly down the dimly lit hallway while Ernest locked the door behind us.

"Well, Jeremy," I said quietly, "where do we start?"

"I've been thinking about that," he said, locking his hands behind his back and striking a professorial pose. "Bart probably wouldn't be able to disappear so often if his access point were in too public a place . . . like out here. If, as I suspect, he's somewhere in the duct-work, he'd come and go through a relatively secluded vent. We should start by looking for vent screens like that."

"Hmm," Ernest said. "That's a good thought, and I think I know just the place."

Most of us took off at a brisk pace, following the handyman, but Danny Singer first placed his battered skateboard gently on the floor and kicked several times before catching up. The soft buzzing of his sealed bearings was punctuated by light staccato double clicks each time the skateboard crossed a seam in the polished floor.

"I've always wanted to do this," he said with satisfaction, sailing past us and weaving gracefully in and out of the planters, waste receptacles, and benches along the way. "Big Lenny wouldn't let us skateboard because of the people."

Ernest led us through the dark and quiet mall, past dozens of shadowy storefront mannequins that looked decidedly more lifelike than they did in the light of day.

"I don't like this *at* all," Tamara said, moving closer to her brother.

"It ain't nothin'," Wallace replied in a whisper. " 'Cept watch out for the ones with fangs." He pulled one side of his black nylon Nike sweat jacket across the bridge of his nose and peered menacingly at Emily, Tamara, and Jeremy. "Vlaa . . . I vant to suck your blood!"

"Stop it!" Tamara said, moving smoothly between Emily and my spinning left wheel.

We came, eventually, to the spot where Big Lenny had been shot earlier that afternoon. Everyone skirted that section of the floor, just as if the big man's blood still lay there in a dark, sticky pool. As we hurried on into the glass elevator at the far corner of the courtyard, a rather disturbing thought occurred to me. For all I knew, Leonard Gordon might have been shot with a .45 army automatic—just like the one tucked in the front of Ernest Boyle's tan work pants. It suddenly felt crowded in the spacious mall elevator.

"In there," Ernest said when the door opened. He nodded toward the dark corridor that led to the public rest rooms and the new mall offices. "We ought probably to be quiet, so to speak, so as not to scare the boy off."

Ernest took a flashlight from his back pocket and pointed it across the floor in front of us as he led the way. No one seemed quite as anxious to go down that hallway as he did, but we all followed in silence, the mall rats keeping close to me on all sides.

"Do you think he, like, did it?" Emily whispered in my ear. Her hand rested gently on my left shoulder.

"Who?" I said without thinking.

"What do you mean, 'who?' " she said, barely breathing the words and pulling me to a stop so that we fell behind the others. She stared into my face, trying to see my eyes in the darkness, as I tried hard to look relaxed. *"I'm* talking about Bart. Who are *you* talking about?"

"Nobody, Emily. I was just daydreaming. I doubt that it was Billy, but I guess that depends on whether we find him with Agent Fredericks's gun, doesn't it?"

"He couldn't keep something like that secret," she said. "I mean, Bart would, like, *have* to brag about lifting an FBI guy's gun. Wouldn't he?"

"I'd think so," I said, stroking several times to catch up with Ernest and the rest of the mall rats as they turned right at the rest rooms and moved past the darkened mall office windows. "But who knows?"

"Look!" Jeremy said in an excited whisper. He was standing between the mall office and a door with STORAGE printed across it, holding the bottom edge of a large air-intake vent screen several inches away from the wall.

The top edge was still fastened but just loosely enough so that the whole panel could be pulled out at the bottom without its being damaged or bent noticeably. When Jeremy pushed it gently back into place, there was no evidence of tampering. There were four screws along the bottom, all of which looked perfectly functional, but when I rolled up and pulled it out myself, I saw that all of them were held in place from behind with chewing gum. The plastic wall sinkers into which they would normally have been secured had simply been removed, leaving only oversized holes in the Sheetrock.

Ernest pointed the flashlight into the dark aluminum tunnel and bent down to peer in. We all did the same. The duct ran straight away from us but downhill at a steep-looking angle—maybe 45 degrees or more. There was a thin layer of dust stuck to the top and sides of the long passage, but the floor of it was clean and polished, undoubtedly scrubbed by Billy's raggedy jeans.

"Okay," I whispered, "so this is how he gets in. How does he get back out?"

"Maybe like climbing back up a slide," Danny offered. "Ya'd have to use your feet against the sides, maybe press up with your back too."

"That would work," Jeremy said softly, "but then the crud would be wiped off the top too. I'll bet he goes out somewhere else . . . probably downstairs."

"Wouldn't matter where he came out, so to speak. Not after everybody'd left." Ernest's light ran out before the dark tunnel did, so we couldn't see the bottom. "I'm sure the blueprints are on file somewhere, but I couldn't get at them right now."

"He's there," Tamara whispered. "I can hear him."

We all held our breath and listened. Aside from a faint rhythmic pulse in the circulation system somewhere, I heard nothing. Blank looks on the other's faces echoed that experience.

"We don't, like, hear anything, Tam," Emily said, gently touching the younger girl's shoulder. "Are you sure?"

"Yeah. Listen." Tamara rocked back and forth between us, holding one finger up in the air as if to point at the distant sound. Her movement matched the faraway mechanical sound perfectly. "There. Do you hear it now?"

"Some machine," Danny said.

"Possibly a circulation fan," Jeremy speculated, "but far too regular to be a human sound."

We all nodded and looked back at Tamara. Her scowl was unmistakable, even in the dim light of the emergency exit sign on the ceiling at the end of the hall.

"It's Bart, you know, the way he rocks back and forth when he's bent out of shape about something." Tamara sat down on the floor between us, crossed her legs, and mimicked Billy's action perfectly. I had never particularly noted his nervous habit, but watching her brought to mind each of my private conversations with Billy. I realized immediately what Tamara apparently already knew: the more distressed he was, the more he rocked in his seat.

"She's right," Wallace said, tugging playfully on one of his sister's cornrow braids. "Never thought about it before, but she's right on."

"Okay," Danny said, handing his skateboard to Jeremy and slipping out of his denim jacket. "I'm going down there."

"Wait," I said.

"Me too," Wallace said, letting his black Nike windbreaker drop off both arms at once and laying it over Tamara's shoulder.

"I, like, want to go too," Emily added, peeling off the first of several colorful layers.

"Now hold on," I said, more loudly than I would have liked. "Let's be smart about this. Ernest, do you have any rope?"

"Sure," he said, shining his flashlight at the storage room door. "Right over here."

He ambled away with the flashlight while I reached behind me for the black canvas pack that contained not only my scratched-up laptop computer but my wallet, some loose change, the latest Rooster Franklin mystery, a blue-and-white bandanna, and a miniature flashlight that I'd always thought might come in handy someday. I switched it on with some satisfaction at having been right after all, only to see the small, tight beam of light strike the corridor wall briefly, fade almost immediately, then disappear.

"Great light, Stickaroo," Danny said, laughing and giving me a friendly slap on the back, "but I think I'll take Soda Speak's flashlight, if ya don't mind."

Wise guy.

"Here, Rollin' Homeboy," Wallace said, pulling a Walkman out of the jacket his sister still had over her shoulder. "Maybe these batteries will work."

They did work. By the time Ernest Boyle returned with a large coil of rope, the tiny flashlight was fully functional, casting a hardy beam of white light that belied its size. Ernest removed the vent cover completely, then ran one end of the rope back out into the food court.

We followed him down the hall and watched as he secured the rope's end to one of the nearby tables and tugged at it with some determination. Many of the tables were freestanding and could be moved about as the size of your party required; others, like the one Ernest had chosen, were bolted to the floor. The boys choked back giggles and the girls both whispered "Gross!" when Ernest squatted down in front of us to double-check his double knot.

"Moon on the mall!" Danny whispered. More giggles broke out, and I shrugged innocently when Ernest turned back toward us, looking puzzled.

By the time we returned to the duct, Jeremy looked decidedly uncomfortable. He fidgeted with Danny's skateboard and glanced nervously at the flurry of preparations around him.

"Someone should probably stay with Stick and watch out for things at this end of the operation," he said finally.

Everyone grinned, and Wallace put a firm hand on his shoulder. "You're the man for the job, Geek," he said. "Besides, you'll need to look after Tamara for me." He glanced at his sister to make sure she understood. "She's not going."

"Neither am I," said Ernest with a chuckle. "If this isn't a job for mall rats, I don't know what is. I'm sure not going down there—not unless I have to rescue someone again, so to speak."

"Well," Jeremy said, sounding unmistakably relieved, "that makes three going and four staying. It's probably better that way—less structural pressure on the aluminum duct work."

"Count again, Jeremy," I said, letting the remaining bundle of rope slide down the dark sheet-metal slope. Stunned silence fell on the small party as I lifted first one lifeless leg, then the other into the opening in the wall beside my wheelchair. "I can't walk, but I can crawl with the best of them."

I stuck the tiny flashlight in my mouth, rolled over on my stomach, and let myself, hand over hand, down into the darkness, hoping fervently that the rope actually reached the bottom . . . wherever or whatever the bottom was.

▽

16

"WELL, STICKMEISTER?" Danny whispered, pointing Ernest's flashlight first one way, then the other. "What now?"

The four of us were nestled together at the bottom of the aluminum incline, with plenty of rope to spare but little room in which to chat comfortably. The duct work was at least level but continued off in two directions: one dark tunnel leading to the courtyard, another straight on toward the main mall, presumably at or about floor level with the shops along the way.

"Let's split up," I said. "Two of us per light."

"I'm going with Stick," Emily said firmly. After the first time, I deliberately avoided letting the small flashlight's beam fall on her. The tight, neon pink, sleeveless T-shirt she wore under all those layers she'd removed up in the hallway left little of her nubile young form to anyone's imagination.

"Okay," I said softly. "Everybody got their beepers?" I received positive responses all around. "One beep means you found him. Two means you're in trouble. The other team will come after you immediately on either one or two beeps. Three means we meet back here. Got it?" Three nods. "Jeremy?"

"Affirmative," came the whispered voice from above.

"Good. Ready?"

"Ah, Rollin' Homeboy?" Wallace said with a grin in his

voice. "I don't mean to rain on your parade, but what if we have to make some turns How will the other team know which way to follow?"

"Mm. Good point."

"Bread crumbs." This time the voice from above was Tamara.

"Not bad, Tam," Emily said. "You, like, got any?"

"Nope."

"In my backpack, Tamara," I said. "Wrap all my loose change up in the bandanna and slide it down here. Ernest? Can you loan us any coins?"

"Sure."

A moment later, the bundle came rocketing down the chute, striking Danny full in the back. After a loud "ouch!" and the giggles that followed, I divided up the change and gave Wallace and Emily each half.

"One coin in the mouth of any new tunnel choice, okay?" More nods and we were finally ready to set out. Any movement at all made the sheet metal flex and groan; even our breathing echoed around us. Finding Billy by sound was out of the question. Since I was already pointing south, in the direction of the mall proper, and since turning around would, for me, have been quite difficult, I volunteered to go that way. Wallace and Danny were already crawling toward the courtyard.

For a while, pulling myself along on my elbows seemed to work fairly well. I kept the flashlight in my teeth, its tight beam swinging back and forth in front of us as I shuffled forward. Emily crawled along behind me, softly humming "Coming Out of the Dark," a fitting tune recorded by Gloria Estefan. We passed one intake vent screen after another, all of which afforded us dim views of the back rooms of as many mall shops. Each screen was securely attached.

By the time we approached what must have been the main mall concourse, my elbows felt like they'd been worked over by a meat grinder, and I would have sworn that the dead weight of my legs had been increasing with every yard of forward movement. I might have pressed on, but Emily called a halt.

"What's this wet stuff?" she asked. I stopped and turned my head back so that the flashlight shone on the floor in front of her. "Gross, Stick! Let me see your elbows. You're, like, bleeding all over."

"So it seems. Okay," I said, pulling the blue-and-white bandanna out of my back pocket and offering it to Emily for her sticky hands, "it looks like I need to take a different approach."

I turned over and sat up—as much as the tight quarters allowed—and tried scooting along backward using my hands. It worked, but the effort would erode even my over-developed shoulder strength before we'd gone very far. And of course I couldn't see where I was going, but then what was there to see but dusty aluminum duct work? I gave the flashlight to Emily and told her not to shine it in my eyes.

We'd only gone several dozen yards or so when she stopped and grabbed my ankle. I'm not sure whether she knew I didn't have any feeling there, but since it effectively stopped my progress, it didn't really matter.

"Look," she said, holding the tiny flashlight up so that it shone past my left shoulder, into the tunnel behind me.

I twisted around enough to see Billy Simpson sitting cross-legged in the middle of a four-duct intersection. He had headphones on and sat rocking to the private tunes. His eyes were glazed over and he was just staring west into the darkness. Despite the fact that Emily was shining our light straight into his face, he didn't seem to be aware of us at all. After I pulled up my legs and struggled to turn around, I took the light from Emily. Billy had apparently been furnishing his little condo by helping himself at several of the mall stores. It appeared, at first glance, that he favored Sears products.

There was a collection of camping gear in the south opening: a foam mattress, a battery-operated fluorescent lantern (which was not turned on), and even a small insulated cooler box. He had a pillow, blankets, and a collection of recent comics, undoubtedly from the nearby bookstore. I kept scanning with the small flashlight as Emily moved into the opening next to me. Behind Billy, in the duct opening that must have gone to Burdines, lay a pile of toys, including a GameBoy and a squirt gun that looked too much like an M16 rifle. On the aluminum floor right in front of the dazed youngster, however, was a real gun. A 10mm government-issue automatic pistol.

"Hey, bud," I said, sliding the weapon away, manually crossing my own legs, and stuffing his pillow behind my back as I slouched against the sheet-metal wall. I turned on the camp lantern and then slipped the personal headphones off his head. "Bill? You in there?"

If he was, he wasn't taking visitors.

Then he lurched upright suddenly, and I hit my head on the low ceiling when my beeper chirped once.

"Sorry," Emily said, clipping hers back on the waist of her now filthy jeans. "I just, like, wanted to let the other guys know."

"Hi, Shh . . . tick," Billy said, unsteadily. His eyes were bloodshot and his breath smelled like imported beer and spicy Polish sausage. So he'd been visiting the Bavarian House too. Figures.

"Wanna foreign brewski?"

"No thanks, Bill. We've got to talk."

"Hokay," he said, pushing himself onto his hands and knees and backing into the "bedroom" area of his compact efficiency apartment. "Whatever you shh . . . ay." After a halfhearted search for his missing pillow, he crumpled up one of the blankets, buried his face in it, and fell promptly and soundly asleep.

It took us an hour to drag Billy out. The nearest vent screen on our level that didn't lead to a locked store was under the small stage in the courtyard. Danny and Wallace discovered it shortly after setting out. It was either that or hoist the unconscious boy up the incline we'd come down. I came out smelling dusty and feeling like I'd just wheeled my way through the Gasparilla Distance Classic in Tampa.

"You guys are groady," Tamara said, brushing gray dust out of her brother's curly black hair. "And Bart smells like he's been eatin' roadkill."

"That's really gross," Jeremy said, "but it smells more like fried bratwurst to me."

Danny, Wallace, and Emily emerged from a second trip through the duct work just as Ernest appeared at the other end of the tunnel with Stanley Fredericks. The tunnel is the hallway connecting the old mall with the courtyard, the food court, and the Maison Blanche store. Stanley looked like he was sleepwalking.

"We put all the stuff back, like ya said," Danny whispered, looking sideways at the approaching FBI man. "And cleaned out the food and the trash. Is he gonna arrest Bart?"

"I don't know, Danny. We'll see, won't we?"

"Here he is," Ernest said when they'd reached the stage. "I think I'd better go crank up Louie's microwave and nuke some instant coffee. Agent Fredericks isn't quite up to speed, so to speak."

"Thanks," Stan said as I handed him my bloodstained bandanna.

"My blood," I said, holding up my elbows as he unwrapped the heavy package. "Your gun?"

"My gun."

Billy Simpson snored contentedly at center stage while the rest of the mall rats sat around watching Stanley examine the pistol. He ran a hand through his graying hair and shook his head sadly.

"Dirty barrel," he said. "One bullet missing." Stanley replaced the clip, carefully using both my handkerchief and his own. "The ballistics lab folks'll say it's almost guaranteed to be the one that killed Leonard Gordon, even though there's never anything but fragments of a Glasier safety slug left to analyze."

"I just thought," I said, a new puzzle dawning on my weary mind, "shouldn't there have been a shell casing, Stan?"

"First thing the OPD looked for, but what would it matter? It would just have my prints on it."

Oh well.

We all sat in silence, listening to Billy snore. Stan slipped the gun into a clear plastic bag, pinched the zipper seal, and took the steaming Styrofoam cup Ernest Boyle was offering.

"Thanks. Don't suppose you shoot Glasiers in that Commander?" he asked, pointing at the Colt in Ernest's belt.

"Nope," Ernest said calmly, offering the pistol to Stan. "Load my own, so to speak. Two-forty-grain military hardballs."

"Just a bad joke," Stanley said, waving away the offered weapon. He took a cautious sip of coffee, swallowed slowly, and sighed. "I've got to take the boy in, Stick. I'm sorry."

"Yeah, Stan. Me too."

▽

17

THE FEDERAL BUILDING was pretty dead at three in the morning. I parked in the waiting room and watched Stanley's finger dance on the almost invisible security push pad near a door that said AUTHORIZED PERSONNEL ONLY. He carried Billy slung unceremoniously over his left shoulder.

"I'll be right back," he said. "Then I'll take you home." Stanley disappeared and the industrial-strength door slammed resolutely behind him.

There was a telephone on the counter at the vacant receptionist's window, several magazines scattered on various chairs and end tables, and a large plate-glass window that looked north toward the Centroplex. The Florida Department of Law Enforcement building was down and to the left; Stan's 10mm automatic was already there. I stared again at the silver three dimensional wall sculpture just outside the crime lab door, but even from five floors up the artist's vision was lost on me.

Directly north across from my window was the Zora Neale Hurston Building, with its blue-domed, fourth-floor sky walk. No one was moving through the colored glass at that hour, and aside from the occasional truck on I-4, the city streets were deserted. As I pulled my faithful laptop computer out of the backpack, I wondered what view Billy would have when he woke up, and what tall tale he would produce to explain our finding him in possession of Stanley's gun.

"He's all tucked in for the night," Stanley said as he returned through the heavy door. "Come on, I'll run you home."

"Thanks, Stan, but I think I'll finish my story and then camp here for the night. Can I use that phone?"

"Sure, but you might as well go home and get some rest. The boy's out for the count."

"I'll be just fine right here. Go home, Stan."

"I'm sorry about the kid, Stick."

"I know. Me too," I said, trying to look more confident than I felt, "but I haven't quite given up on him yet."

"You have a thing for long shots, Stick," Stanley said with a quiet laugh, "I'll give you that; but I'm going back to bed. Good night."

Mm. Not hardly.

The stories went together pretty well, except that I was getting tired and kept having lapses in my concentration where I suddenly found myself staring out the window toward the east, singing "O-oh say, can you see, by the dawn's early light," and tapping out the rhythm on my keyboard with my right index finger. That was disconcerting. Each time I caught myself doing it I felt more ridiculous, deleted the gibberish from my screen, and went back to work. Until I noticed that the gibberish wasn't quite the random nonsense I had thought.

```
79ijn,79ijn,
```

It was the same six characters, every time: seven, nine, the letters *i, j, n,* and then a comma. Still gibberish. Still nonsense. But hauntingly consistent nonsense. Why?

I looked at the computer keyboard and then intentionally poked out the strangely recursive series, automatically humming "The Star Spangled Banner" as I did so. The characters formed a *Z*-like pattern across the right side of my keyboard, but otherwise made no apparent sense.

"What is that famous symbol?" asked George Hamilton in one of my favorite movies, *Zorro, the Gay Blade*.

"Why eet eez zee number two, señor," the thankful Mexican peasant replied.

"No, no," the dismayed masked hero pleaded. "Look again. It is the letter *Z!*"

"Pardon, señor, but in school they teach my daughter that eet eez zee number two."

The memory brought a smile to my face, but no solution to my puzzle. Why was I absentmindedly punching out a *Z*-shaped pattern on my computer keyboard . . . and to the tune of "The Star Spangled Banner"? Six characters. Six beats to each musical phrase. So what?

I set the laptop on the nearest magazine-strewn end table and backed away from it. Maybe if I looked at it from a distance. Suddenly I thought of the alien musical notes in *Close Encounters of the Third Kind*. It was a code! But a code to what? I could see the headlines on all the tabloids: ALIENS CONTACT FLA REPORTER THROUGH LAPTOP COMPUTER.

Maybe if I moved around, woke up. One halfhearted rolling pace across the small waiting room, however, was all it took. When it hit me, I laughed out loud. I knew Stanley's pass code to the AUTHORIZED PERSONNEL ONLY door in the room's west wall!

The innocuous security keypad was part and parcel with the grass-cloth wall covering, and had I not watched Stanley operate it, I would not likely have noticed it at all. Closer examination revealed a small, twenty-button panel with four evenly spaced rows of five keys each, numbered sequentially from 1 to 20. It was almost too easy. If I had somehow correctly absorbed the configuration of Stanley's dancing finger, there were only two possible access codes.

The *Z* pattern I'd been typing would fit on the keypad in only two places. That was most fortuitous. Assuming that each key could only be used once and that my rusty college math still served me (both significant assumptions), the normal permutations of a six-number code out of a twenty-number field would run just under 28 million. As it was, the only possible winning combinations were 2, 4, 8, 12, 16, 18 and 3, 5, 9, 13, 17, 19.

Well, just knowing should have been enough. But it

wasn't. I hadn't a clue what was behind that door—except maybe Billy, somewhere—but the urge to open it and find out was irresistible. I tried to rationalize my compunction by calling it natural reporter's curiosity, but knew that was, as my mall rat friends would have said, bogus. I was just a big kid who couldn't resist trying to get into something that was clearly off limits.

After retrieving my computer and returning it to my backpack, I started to reach for the keypad, intending to try the code that began with the number 2. That's when the proverbial rub occurred to me. What little I knew of business security systems—a knowledge gleaned while doing a week-long series on security guards in Melbourne and Palm Bay—included the memory of something a road-patrol security officer had said. "The *better* systems," he'd noted while letting us into the vacant winter home of a New York City couple, "will automatically signal the security office if an incorrect code is entered."

Mm.

Okay, so the Federal Bureau of Investigation probably had one of the better systems. Still, I decided to look at the bright side of things. A fifty-fifty chance sure beats one in 28 million, and I would, of course, apply tried-and-true scientific technique to narrowing down my choice.

Ink-a, bink-a, bottle-a-inka . . .

It was, indeed, a close call—and to think that I'd almost used the "two" code. I gripped the doorknob with my left hand and warmed up by humming a couple bars of "The Star Spangled Banner"—just in case Stanley's tempo had anything to do with the outcome—before jumping in finger first. I concluded my *Z* by hitting the number nineteen key with a jaunty flair and saying: "No! It is the letter *Z* . . . for El Zorro!"

Bueno! The invisible latch clicked, vibrating the stainless-steel doorknob. I turned it hard to the left, pulled open the heavy door, and rolled into the dim hallway beyond. Some inner voice warned me that what I was doing was probably not too smart, but then I've never claimed to be a genius. But I sure could carry a tune.

Ho-osea can you see . . .

The large room through the glass wall on my right was divided into cubicle-sized offices, each with its own computer terminal. When I came to one with a black plastic J. DRAKE placard on the outer wall near the opening that passed for the office's door, I rolled right in. Jody and I went way back; well, at least a year back, that is. We were buddies . . . almost. Surely Agent Drake wouldn't mind if I just took a peek at her computer. That's when I noticed that my heart was pounding hard enough to shake the building—or at least my wheelchair.

Down, Simba.

All the terminals were up; that is, they apparently remained turned on at all times. Whether or not I could actually access any information was another matter. When I touched the space bar, the automatic moiré, or screen-saver patterns, disappeared and the amber cursor blinked expectantly in the dark screen's upper left corner. What I needed was a menu.

After experimenting unsuccessfully for several moments, I started searching Jody's shelves and drawers for a system manual. When I found one and looked up the menu command, it turned out (as many puzzles do) to be quite simple. I depressed the Control and the question mark keys simultaneously and a main menu screen appeared in crisp, clear amber letters on the monitor in front of me.

Most of the selections meant nothing to me, but "State Search" and "National Search" looked promising. I typed the number 6 and hit the Enter key.

PLEASE WAIT. . . .

The bright amber instruction lasted scant seconds, and was replaced with a question.

WHAT STATE DO YOU WISH TO SEARCH?

Florida, I typed, then hit the Enter key.

PLEASE WAIT. . . .

This time the wait was slightly longer, but in less than thirty seconds, the computer questioned me again.

```
BY WHAT PARAMETER DO YOU WISH TO SEARCH?
          (A) NAME
          (B) ALIAS
          (C) ADDRESS
          (D) OFFENSE
          (E) PHYSICAL DESCRIPTION
          (F) RETURN TO MAIN MENU
```

It was just like being a kid with an unlimited charge account at the candy store. I punched the *A* key and hit Enter once again.

```
PLEASE ENTER SEARCH NAME, LAST NAME FIRST:
```

Foster, Nicholas

```
SEARCHING. PLEASE WAIT. . . .
```

All of a sudden, there I was—age, weight, eyes, hair, address, everything. It even listed Stick as an alias. Also included were several old traffic violations and an impressive list of charges, which included: interfering with a federal investigation, resisting arrest, failure to comply, carrying and discharging a handgun without a permit, aggravated assault, and unnecessary violence.

Mm.

Fortunately the file had been amended to read:

```
ALL CHARGES DROPPED. See file #003-263476-2128.
```

Still, it made me look like, well, as Wallace would say, "a *bad* dude." Sam would have laughed out loud.

My next search was a late acquaintance.

Gordon, Leonard

```
PLEASE WAIT. . . .
```

Big Lenny's file was not particularly significant; that is, aside from a number of minor incidents—including several botched citizen's arrest attempts and threatening a door-to-door salesman with a loaded .357 revolver—the big man had never been in any kind of trouble. Okay, so he was shot, apparently, just for being an overweight, pompous, royal pain in the butt. *Good* men have died for less.

I figured Sam's file would contain a couple of drunk-and-disorderly-type notations, but I was wrong. She wasn't in there at all. Upon reflection, it made sense. To merit an FBI file, one probably had to be charged with a federal offense. In any case, I was relieved that my new bride was not on the Ten Most Wanted list.

Ernest Boyle had an official record because he was a registered handgun owner, with a permit to carry a concealed weapon. To my great surprise, his file also included a notation indicating his status as an ex-Green Beret. Soda Speak? Who'd have thought? Fred Lucas's file was even stranger. It listed his name but no additional information save the enigmatic notation:

```
FWPP EYES ONLY.
```

Mm.

There was no such lack of data in Luigi Leone's FBI file. It was five screens long, containing detailed records of the most mundane aspects of his daily life. There was a list of friends and acquaintances with dated notations about social visits, there was a list of phone numbers with dates and cross-referenced file numbers, and there were even notes about the village in Sicily where he was born. In all that data, there was not the slightest indication that Louie had so much as broken the speed limit. I found the whole idea of that file offensive . . . but then what did I know about fighting organized crime? Nothing.

Just because the very idea was so ludicrous, I tried to call up a file on the late Martha Galliger. Of course, there was none. I looked at my watch. It was nearly six o'clock, and I had already pushed my luck; still, just one more . . .

Galliger, Constance

`PLEASE WAIT. . . .`

Good night, nurse!

▽

18

EVERY FAMILY HAS its skeletons, I suppose, but discovering that the youngest daughter of a wealthy and proper Orlando citrus grower was something of a rebellious high school hellion was quite amusing. Our saintly and distinguished Sister Constance Galliger had a long string of teenage offenses, including destruction of public property (mailboxes and city fountains), shoplifting (often and anything), and even grand theft auto.

My, my, my. Were we trying to get Daddy's attention, or what?

Well, Daddy Galliger had apparently been kept busy paying people off and smoothing ruffled feathers because, like my own brief file, Constance's had "Charges Dropped" after each entry. At any rate, 1949 must be particularly memorable for our Miss Constance. It was her senior year . . . and she was busted four times.

My fascination almost made me forget being nervous.

"Magic season tickets for how much? No way!"

The voice and, of course, the ceiling lights all coming on at once startled me so badly that I almost tried to stand up. I fumbled frantically to get back to the main menu and clear the screen, at the same time wondering how to sneak a wheelchair out past a room full of trained federal agents. What on earth were they doing, coming to work at six o'clock in the morning? What kind of a fascist government did we have anyway?

"Yes way. I talked to the man himself."

"Well, yeah, I'll call him. Are you sure they're not counterfeit or something?"

"Corporate freebies. He gets them free, hates basketball, and loves to make a fast buck."

The once dim and quiet room was all lights and shuffling humanity as I desperately tried to figure out how to turn on the screen-saver moiré. Anyone seeing the active black-and-amber monitor screen would automatically know I'd been doing more than simply breaking and entering on government property. The voices, more of them every second, were getting closer.

When I saw the tops of two brown-haired heads coming along the outside of Jody's cubicle wall, I had to fight not to pass out. My heart pounded like a jackhammer and my mind was going blank. At the last second, I spun Agent Drake's office chair around so that the seat back blocked any newcomer's view of the terminal screen, tipped my chair back into a wheelie against the wall near the doorless cubicle opening, let my chin drop down on my chest, and did my best fast asleep act.

"Hey! Who in blazes are you, and what are you doing in here?"

I jerked my head up suddenly, blinking my eyes as if startled completely and lifting my elbows up off the tops of my wheels. With the braking pressure of my elbows removed, the big wheels shot forward, away from the wall, dumping me over backwards in a heap on the floor. The effect was perfect.

"Oh, I'm so sorry. Are you all right?"

"Hey," said the second guy, "I know him. It's that newspaper writer . . . Foster, isn't it?"

"Oh, crap! He's Stan and Jody's friend."

I shook my head and rubbed my eyes while the abashed agents tripped over themselves trying to right my wheelchair and lift me back into it. I let them, of course, remaining as limp and helpless as I could. By that time a crowd of six or eight people had gathered, and several razzed the first agent for trying to "kill the poor handicapped guy."

"Water?" I said, still looking as befuddled as possible, and someone ran off like my life depended on it. I blinked some more, moaned, and rubbed the back of my head for good measure. "Ouch."

"I'm really sorry, Mr. Foster," the young agent said again. "I didn't mean to startle you. I mean, I didn't know . . ."

"Call me Stick. And it's okay," I said, readjusting my feet on the footrests and generally straightening myself out in the chair, stopping occasionally to rub the back of my head. "I drove over with Stanley and a young prisoner early this morning and thought I'd wait for Jody."

The waterboy returned, pushed his way past the concerned faces, and I thanked him before sipping slowly from the red plastic cup. "I wanted to be around when the boy woke up, and thought Jody might take me back so I could talk to him. Stanley was up all night. . . ."

"Oh, no sweat," said the agent who was obviously still mortified about knocking me out of my wheelchair, "Jody's in the field, but I'll take you to holding myself."

The small crowd parted like the Red Sea, several agents patting me on the back and complimenting me on my mall stories. The fact that I was in a totally restricted area no longer seemed to trouble anyone.

I'd like to thank the members of the Academy. . . .

We passed through several more security doors, each more elaborate than the one before, and all requiring both a code and a pass card. Billy was still sleeping it off, and the young agent said I could wait there near his cell if I wanted. "There aren't any chairs back here," he said apologetically before catching himself, "but, ah, then you don't need one, do you?"

We laughed, but I declined the offer, asking instead whether, if I rolled up to the Burger Man on Colonial, they'd let me back in later.

"Sure. No sweat."

I used the phone in the outer lobby to dump my stories before rolling several blocks north for a fast-food breakfast.

When I returned, I phoned Sam at her office and tried to give her a toned-down version of the night's events, but even Ben "Good News" Dawson couldn't have made the calamitous evening go down any better. Sam was appalled, and said so, but we were both very careful about how we reacted to each other. We were learning. . . .

Stanley was back at work when I returned, and he accompanied me back to holding. He never said anything about my little adventure in the office area, and I sure didn't bring it up, but something in the way he carried himself told me he was saving it up for me later. He did agree, grudgingly, to let me try talking to Billy first. For his part, Billy didn't seem particularly interested in either the egg sandwich or the french toast sticks I brought back to him, but he sipped slowly on the orange juice, making sour faces and shuddering with each swallow. I had to tell him why he felt so bad and how he'd gotten where he was. He couldn't remember.

I also had to ask him how it was that we'd found him with Stanley Fredericks's 10mm automatic.

"I found it, Stick, honest."

Right.

"Come on, bud. You gotta work with me here; you're in way over your head. Sam and I will do everything we can for you, but lying now will only make things worse."

"I didn't steal the stupid gun!" he shouted, immediately regretting it and clutching both temples between his palms. "Oooh."

"Big Lenny died, Bill," I said quietly.

He looked first at Stanley, then back at me. His eyebrows momentarily furled into a question, but then he spat out a "pah" the way the mall rats often do when expressing derision.

"Do you really expect me to care?" he said shortly. "That guy hated my guts . . . treated me like dirt." Then, either because he was trying to be clever or because his foggy brain was putting the picture together for the first time, his eyes widened suddenly. "He was shot?"

I nodded.

"Same gun?"

I nodded again.

"Crap!" He left the bars and stomped around the cell for a moment, slapping his hips with the palms of his hands. Then, slipping down onto the lone bunk, he put his elbows on his knees and his head in his hands and started rocking from side to side. He didn't even attempt to hide the fact that he was crying.

Maybe he was innocent. And maybe I wouldn't win that Academy Award after all. . . .

▽

19

I TALKED WHILE the malls rats ate the pizza I'd paid for with the last of my pocket money. (It was time to hit the lady lawyer up for another loan till payday.) I'd asked Louie to join us, so he sat there chain-smoking, glancing back occasionally to check on his hired help. Like my previous adolescent posse ideas, the kids loved my new one.

"I want to be the official timer!" Jeremy said, waving his multifunction calculator watch.

"I'll, like, stay here with Stick," Emily said.

"I'll play Big Lenny," Tamara said, puffing out her cheeks and holding her arms out from her sides.

"I want to be the unknown guy," Wallace said enthusiastically. "Alias: Homey the Mysterious!"

"Okay," Danny said, "that does it. I'm Bart and Stick Guy and Louie play themselves. Positions, everyone. Quiet on the set, people! And . . . roll it!"

Louie stood behind the stainless-steel pizza counter, leaned forward on his elbows, and watched with some amusement as we role-played the first of our scenarios. As "unknown" wasn't featured, Wallace joined Emily, Danny, and me as we attempted to re-create the scene at the lunch table just before Big Lenny was shot. While Jeremy manned his stopwatch, and Tamara headed down the escalator, I repeated my presentation about the beepers and the rap song. When we got to the practice part, Danny (playing Billy Simpson) backed away from the table and drifted slowly toward the escalator.

Emily, Wallace, and I started around the food court—this time whispering the song—trying to follow our original course.

"Over there!" Louie called out. "Turn between those two tables and come this way. Right! That's it!"

The Palmetto Plaza lunch crowd watched us with no small curiosity, as did my tired and reluctant friend, Stanley Fredericks. It was his job to play all the extras, the considerable crowd that had flowed up the escalator and lined the glass balcony railing to watch our original performance. When we seemed to have covered the appropriate route and sung approximately the same number of verses as before, we looked at Louie and he nodded in agreement.

"Okay," I said. "On three. One . . . Two . . . Three . . ."

"BANG!" we all shouted at once.

Below us, in the courtyard, Danny had strolled south toward the main mall, then turned and headed back in our direction. He was approaching Tamara, who was waddling toward him with her cheeks puffed out, when we shouted "Bang." Danny enhanced the minidrama by aiming his right arm at Tamara's chest and making his shoulder jerk back from the recoil; she, in turn, clutched her heart dramatically and collapsed backward onto the floor. Passersby looked decidedly uncomfortable about the whole affair.

Danny kept moving in our direction at a steady pace and started up the escalator as the rest of us moved toward the balcony to join the "crowd" straining to see what had transpired below. He had to walk right past us before he headed down the hallway to the rest rooms, the mall offices, and the vent that led to Billy's lair. Seconds after he disappeared, we heard him shout, "Cut!"

Jeremy pushed the appropriate button on his watch and Danny appeared back in the food court almost immediately. "That's a wrap on scene one, people!" Danny said coming toward us with a wry smile. "Let's set the next scene. Go, go, go . . . time is money!"

"There's, like, no way, is there, Stick?" Emily said, her hand coming to rest on my shoulder. "Bart, like, couldn't have just walked right by all of us, could he?"

"What do you think, Stan?" I said, turning to the somber-looking FBI agent.

"Not very likely, anyway," he said. "How long did that take, Jeremy?"

"Thirteen minutes, forty-three point seven, six, two, five—"

"That's close enough!" Emily said, swatting him with the back of her hand. Jeremy grinned, shrugged his shoulders, and pushed his heavy glasses back up his nose.

"Never happened," Danny said flatly. "Let's try the next one. Places everyone! Lights! Camera! And . . . action!"

Tamara, who had just staggered off the escalator, still clutching her chest, looked disappointed at missing our brief discussion but did a wonderful impression from *Monty Python and the Holy Grail* as she started toward the down side of the moving stair.

"It's just a flesh wound!" she said. "I'm feeling much better!"

We ran the same scene again; but this time, instead of coming up the escalator, Danny crossed the courtyard the other way, came up in the glass elevator, and circled the imaginary crowd by hugging the wall until he got to the hallway by the pizza shop.

"Better," Stanley said when Danny called it a wrap.

"Only two and a half minutes longer," Jeremy added.

"Yeah," Emily said sadly, "Bart, like, *maybe* coulda done it that way."

"I don't think so."

It was Louie. He pulled up a chair and automatically lit a cigarette.

"The boy would have walked right in front of my face either way," he said, gesturing across the counter with his hand, and Mr. Bart is not easy to miss with that bright yellow head of hair!"

Mm.

"Okay," I said, looking at Wallace. "You're up, Homey the Mysterious. Let's try Billy's scenario."

"Places everyone!" Danny said, "quiet on the set . . . and let's get this in one take!"

This time, when Danny backed, pouting, away from our table, he walked casually around the food court in the opposite direction, disappearing into the hallway without ever passing in front of Louie's shop.

Lord, let this work. . . .

Wallace looked up from the north mouth of the tunnel, waiting for Stanley's signal. Just as we neared the "Bang!" finale, Stan waved and Wallace advanced on his little sister. Tamara died well, and Homey the Mysterious sauntered casually across the courtyard and into the see-through elevator. Again, the walk-by shooter bypassed most of the crowd but had to pass immediately in front of Luigi Leone's pizza shop. And this time it could have been anyone, someone who might not cause a second glance . . . or even a first.

Mm.

We all followed Wallace down the short hallway, around the corner, and watched as he looked both ways before pulling out the bottom of the vent screen and reaching up underneath.

"Ouch!" Danny's voice echoed up from the bottom of the dark aluminum tunnel when my handkerchief full of coins struck him for the second time in as many days. "That's a bull's-eye and a wrap, people! We have a blockbuster on our hands!"

"Same time!" Jeremy said enthusiastically. "I mean, within half a minute. And from the shot to the drop was less than three."

"And," Emily added in a burst of sudden inspiration, "with, like, the 'phones on, Bart probably wouldn't even have heard the shot—I mean, we hardly did."

The remaining mall rats and I breathed a simultaneous sigh of relief; even Stanley's face showed the first signs of finally allowing himself to share a bit of our fragile hopes for Billy's innocence.

According to his agitated account of his actions after leaving the food court, Billy'd sneaked into his private bolt hole, stopped at the bottom of the slope long enough to dig his radio headphones out of the right front pocket of his ratty camo pants, get them untangled and installed in his ears, and get himself tuned in. Finding a decent station had taken, he thought, a couple of minutes. He had just bent forward on all fours, he insisted, ready to crawl away, when the gun came hurtling down the aluminum chute, striking him on the back of his left leg. (He even showed us a bruise.)

"Hope deferred makes the heart sick," my dad always quoted King Solomon as having written in the thirteenth chapter of Proverbs, "but when dreams come true at last, there is life and joy." There was, if not the realization of dreams, at least a definite glimmer of hope. Now all we needed to do was find Homey the Mysterious.

I suddenly felt extremely tired, barely able to remain upright in my wheelchair. As the hallway around me began to blur and spin, my last conscious thought was something about learning to pace myself.

▽

20

I WOKE UP in my own bed, alone. The phone on the end table was ringing and the alarm clock told me it was either midnight or noon. Given that the ceiling light was off and I could still see the old white Westclock, I figured it was probably the latter. As annoying as the persistent telephone was, it was preferable to the hysterical voice that pierced my left ear when I finally answered it.

"Yes, Mrs. Simpson."

Lord, help me.

"I know he's in the Juvenile Detention Center, Mrs. Simpson."

What did I do to deserve this?

"Yes, Mrs. Simpson. Please calm down a little bit."

Fat chance.

"No, I'm sure he's fine, and no, I don't think he shot anyone."

Hope springs eternal.

"Yes. Yes. Yes, I'll talk with him."

Please, please, please hang up and leave me alone.

"No, I don't think you should go visit him just now."

Lord, spare Billy this. He's having a tough enough time as it is.

"Yes, I promise I'll see him and get back to you, Mrs. Simpson."

How's the next millennium for you?

"You're welcome. Good-bye."

And good riddance.

Along with the *Sentinel* (opened to my page three "New Nick Foster Gang Nabs Street Thugs" article), there were two notes on the breakfast table. One was a stern rebuke from Sam, ending, fortunately, with kinder words of an offer for the use of her Mustang (if I could find a way in to town to get it), and a moderate but all-caps admonition to eat something. The other was a brief note from Stanley, which included the name of a contact person at Juvey who would be looking for me and would let me in to see Billy. The boy's transfer from the Federal Building had, apparently, gone fairly well.

After a series of phone calls that included the OPD (for a copy of the "accident" report on my Monte), my auto insurance agent (she wasn't thrilled), and my beloved solicitor (for advice about getting good representation for Billy), I assembled and burned something resembling an omelet and ate it with a side order of Breyer's mint chocolate chip ice cream. I banged out an article—again featuring my mall rat posse, and highlighting their determined efforts on behalf of their incarcerated friend—and dumped it on Ben Dawson's desk by plugging the handy laptop in to the kitchen phone cord.

Good News wasn't as soft a touch as Randy White, my former editor at the *Melbourne Suncoaster,* but it occurred to me that since my classic Monte had been ravaged in the line of duty, the paper should, at least, provide me with a rental car until mine was rehabed and returned. Ben hemmed and hawed, but in the end decided that he probably didn't want word getting around Orlando that he had his new ace reporter pounding the beat in an Orange County Special Services' handicapped shuttle bus.

At three o'clock, an employee of National Car Rental rang my doorbell and handed me the keys to a brand-new red Cutlass Supreme, complete with an AM/FM stereo cassette, left-hand controls, and no backseat. Five minutes later, with one of my K. T. Oslin tapes stress-testing the Oldsmobile's speaker system, I was on my way to the body shop to retrieve my cellular car phone. I wasn't surprised to discover that Willis Dent hadn't bothered to unscrew my antenna but was relieved when one of the mechanics was able to extract the broken stub without damaging anything else. After a stop at Southeast Electronics for a replacement, I was officially back in business.

I used the main mall entrance and rolled directly to Jacob's Clothiers. Fred Lucas wasn't going to like what I had to say, but I had a feeling he was going to talk to me. Unless I was greatly mistaken, it was a matter of life or death.

On my way into the store I nearly ran into a stern-looking Constance Galliger.

"Why, hello, Mr. Foster," she said, shifting her shawl to her left arm and extending her right hand. "I've been following your little adventures, and I must say that you do seem to attract more than your share of calamities!"

"It sure seems that way, doesn't it? By the way, Miss Galliger, I've been meaning to call you. Would you mind if I brought the kids out to your place some afternoon? I thought maybe they'd like the chance to fish or swim; you know, just get out of the city for a little while."

Her reaction was more interesting than I'd thought it might be. The initial flash of what could have been anger, snobbery, or fear in her eyes lasted only a split second. A simple request of Christian hospitality from one church member to another was not something one in her position could refuse with any degree of grace. Okay, so I had the church lady over an ecclesiastical barrel and I knew it. Sue me.

"Why, of course," Constance said, with remarkable restraint and a nearly believable smile. "Just give me a little warning and perhaps I'll bake them some cookies."

"That would be wonderful," I said, wondering suddenly at the wisdom of sparring with such a formidable woman. Knowing something of Constance's secret adolescence, though, made me feel more emboldened than I might have only a day earlier. "It means a lot for these kids to see that not every adult hates them just because they're young and rambunctious," I said, charging on heedlessly. "You know kids; they all go through these stages . . . and most of them grow out of it and turn out just fine."

"I'm sure they do," Sister Galliger said with a curious edge to her voice. "Now I really must go. Good day, Mr. Foster."

"Good-bye. And thanks. . . ."

"I tip my proverbial hat to you."

I turned to find Fred Lucas holding his stylish pipe in one hand and a pair of white linen women's gloves in the other.

"I wish you'd been here a few minutes ago to handle my little exchange with Miss Constance."

"Hello, Fred. Problems in retail land?"

"Only that the customer is always right. Look at these."

He handed me the gloves and shook his head disparagingly.

"One of them's dirty," I said. "So?"

"So, Laura—our newest salesperson—sold them to her the other day. Miss Constance obviously uses them, soils them, and returns them, demanding a refund. She claims they were dirty before she purchased them. Can you imagine? An old lady who could buy and sell this whole chain several times over pulling a cheap trick like that; I mean, the gloves only cost six ninety-five in the first place!"

"Are you on alone, Fred?"

"No. Laura's in the back. Why?"

"We need to chat. Can you take a break?"

"Well, sure. Nothing's moving here today. I'll get Laura out of the back and tell her we're going upstairs for a cup of coffee."

"Ah, Fred, maybe that's not such a good idea. Can we use the back? This probably ought to be somewhere private."

Fred Lucas's face underwent an instantaneous metamorphosis. The calm, slightly haughty composure disappeared, and the smooth, steady pipe hand began to waver. He desperately searched my eyes for signs that I was just Nick Foster the reporter, not a wraith come from the shadows to haunt him. Fred Lucas found no such reassurance, and he hastened to the stock room, asked the young sales clerk to watch the floor, and motioned for me to join him. Before closing the door behind us, he surveyed the store and stared intently out toward the mall concourse. When he came at last and sat heavily in the manager's office chair, Fred Lucas looked at me again.

"What do you want?"

"I want to know who killed Martha Galliger and Lenny Gordon."

"Everyone who reads the Orlando paper knows that," Fred said steadily. "What do you want from me?"

"Anything you can tell me that will help—"

"I already told you—" he interrupted, but I waved him quiet.

"Well, Fred, there's this matter of who you are and who you're hiding from that's sort of a barrier between us, you know? It's a trust thing."

Jacob's senior salesclerk lost all semblance of composure, lurched to his feet, and paced the small storeroom, waving his arms over his head and muttering to himself.

"I knew I shouldn't have trusted them! I'm dead. Even after all these years, I'm dead." He turned suddenly back toward me and spoke with solemn desperation. "Why are you doing this? I have nothing but this job."

"I'm in a corner too, Fred . . . or whoever you really are. I don't particularly care why you're in the Federal Witness Protection Program, and I don't particularly want to let your secret out of the bag, but I won't sit still while Billy Simpson's young life goes in the dumper over a murder he didn't commit. If you know anything at all that might help me, you'd better tell me now. If I dig around anymore by myself, I'm likely to draw the attention of people you'd just as soon have looking the other way."

▽

21

IGNORANCE AND INEXPERIENCE are two faces of a worthless coin. No matter how many times you flip it, you come up a loser. I had Fred Lucas right in my hands, squirming helplessly. But Fred Lucas—or maybe Homey the Mysterious for all I knew—had been around the block far more times than I. He led me down the garden path while pleading for his life and promising to meet me somewhere, anywhere, other than his place of employment. After he whined, cajoled, and all but assured me everything short of a written statement, I agreed to meet him after his shift was over. Besides, I needed to visit Billy anyway.

Wrong. Buzz.

Laura Callahan's eyes told the whole story when I said I'd come back to meet Fred and asked whether he was finished up in the back. Her unnecessary words only added insult to injury.

"He left right after you did, Mr. Foster."

"Just call me Stick, okay?"

Or just call me Bonehead. Same thing.

"Sure, Stick. Well, Fred left in kind of a hurry. He said he'd be back to close out the register, but we were supposed to start that ten minutes ago. I've never done it by myself; what do you think I should do?"

"Give me Fred's phone number and home address, and

then call the manager. Tell her Fred Lucas doesn't exist anymore."

"What?"

"Sorry. Just tell the manager what happened. She'll tell you what to do."

There was, of course, no answer at Fred's number. I called on my way to the Conway address. A neighbor came out while I was pounding without much hope on the apartment door.

"Big white truck came about an hour ago," the shirtless, hairy, and overweight man said. "Strangest thing. One minute Mr. Lucas lives here happy as a lark for three years . . . the next minute he packs up lock, stock, and barrel and moves off without giving me no notice."

"Are you the manager?"

"Five years," he said proudly. "Never seen nothin' like it. One of Mr. Lucas's friends in the white coveralls even give me five hundred bucks to square things with the landlord. Shoot, Mr. Lucas just paid next month's rent, and he paid a month's advance *and* a damage deposit when he moved in. That's more than any landlord needs, eh?"

"I'd think so," I said, too busy mentally kicking myself to care.

"Finally gonna get that big-screen remote," the man with the fuzzy belly said with a wink. "Whatcha think?"

"Your lucky day," I said, walking away.

Nick "Bonehead" Foster. Has kind of a ring to it. . . .

When I got home, there were three stern faces waiting around my kitchen table. Fortunately, Sam's face was the least stern of the lot. Stan Fredericks and Jody Drake, however, hadn't come for tea. As dense as I can be sometimes, it didn't take a genius to sort out what had happened between the time I walked naively away from Fred Lucas at Jacob's Clothiers and my present Kodak moment. On top of all that, I was hungry.

"Hi, guys," I said, opening the refrigerator, retrieving the butter dish and the strawberry preserves. "Mah-jongg, right?"

I didn't look back at them but concentrated on the loaf of

iced cinnamon raisin bread by the toaster. It was dead quiet while I plastered two slices of the sticky bread with butter and preserves; even while I sprinkled Cheerios on top of that, no one spoke. After I slapped the two works of culinary art together, I turned to face the silent music. Same faces, same storm brewing. All I needed now was another call from Billy's mother.

"Want one?" I said, offering up my all-time-favorite multi-food-group health snack. "I call it Strawberry Delight."

Tough room.

"Do you want me to lose my retirement, Stick? Is that it?"

So Stanley's voice still worked. Okay, it sounded more like the old "agent god" I first met out on Mosquito Lagoon almost a year before, but that was pretty reasonable under the circumstances. I bit into my sandwich on the assumption that Stan's question was rhetorical. One bad thing about my heavenly strawberry treats is not being able to keep the icing out of one's facial hair. But I was among friends. . . .

"You almost got Stan fired flat out today, Stick," Jody said. "And neither one of us is off the hook, not by a long shot. You'd better have a convincing explanation for how you broke in to the office."

"I do," I said, picking chunks of white icing off the corners of my mustache, "but you should really have seen how I got back out. Man, I was *great!*"

"We heard," Stan said coldly.

Jody, to her credit, tried extremely hard to retain her composure. To my credit, however, she started to waver almost immediately. Sam watched in total amazement as I propped my wheelchair back against the refrigerator and acted out my charade. When I let it roll out from under me and collapsed on the kitchen floor, Jody lost it altogether. Stan held out longer, but when I rubbed the back of my head and moaned, both agents slid off their seats and sat on the linoleum, holding their ribs.

"Stick!" Sam protested. "You didn't."

Stan and Jody just nodded their heads, tears running down their faces.

"That's shameless!" Sam said, when I rubbed my head

some more and reenacted my request for water, but a growing smile meant the last of the tension was finally breaking.

"I'm sorry," I said at last. "I've really been a bonehead, but I never meant to get you guys in trouble. I never even meant to go back there; it was an accident—but man, it was a rush and a half!"

"Those guys are in more trouble than we are," Stan said finally. "I'd almost have given my retirement to see you pull that off!"

"You just *had* to use *my* office? The code's been changed, of course," Jody said, "but how on earth did you get through the lobby door?"

They listened skeptically, shaking their heads throughout my only slightly embellished tale of absentminded recall. Sam poured pink lemonade and interrupted several times to say, "Stick, are you nuts?" and "*What* were you thinking?" Her questions were, of course, rhetorical. She knew the answers long before she agreed to marry me. In the end, as my engrossing tale wound down to its thrilling conclusion, inspiration struck again.

At first, Stan and Jody balked, but eventually—emboldened by my own thespian heroics—they agreed to take me in, cuffed hand and foot like a serial killer, and throw me in the lockup for the night.

"After all," Sam said, nailing down the last of my impeccable reasoning, "you want your superiors to know how seriously you are taking this inexcusable breach of security. An example needs to be made of *someone*, and it's either you guys or Bozo here!"

There was no need for a vote, and while Sam (and half the apartment complex) looked on in awe, Stan and Jody pushed my stainless steel–shackled form out to the gray Chrysler sedan and unceremoniously threw me in the backseat. After carefully putting my backpack up front, Jody folded my wheelchair and put it in the trunk. The last thing I saw as we drove away was Sam shrugging her shoulders at the other spectators before returning to the apartment and closing the front door.

What a remarkable woman.

* * *

"I just heard that I'd be seeing you again!" said the night jailer when I was rolled in, but he did a double take at the body shackles. "Did he try to give you guys the slip too?" he said to Stan and Jody, laughing nervously and opening up one of the cell doors. When Stan pushed me into the cell, jerked up on the back of my chair, and dumped me out onto the painted concrete floor, the young agent with the keys nearly swallowed his tongue.

"Jeez, Fredericks! You trying to break his neck? Take it easy!"

"The gimp thinks he can make fools out of us and then waltz away like one of Jerry's poster kids," Stan said with considerably more biting severity than we'd made him rehearse in the car.

Mm.

"Here," he said bluntly, slamming the cell door and shoving my chair at the young man before him. "He won't be needing this tonight!"

As I struggled into a sitting position (falling sideways against the bars a couple of times for good measure), the horrified jailer blinked in astonishment. "Aren't you going to take off the restraints?" he said, his eyes darting from Jody to Stan and back.

"Hmm," Jody said, checking her pockets with no real enthusiasm. "Did I give you those keys, Stan?"

"No," Stanley said without checking, "but I'm sure they'll turn up by morning."

"Morning?" I asked with sincerity. We'd never rehearsed anything about "morning." But the show had to go on. . . .

"Hey, guys," I pleaded, twisting around and squeezing my face through the bars at the level of their knees, "I said I was sorry. I didn't mean to get anybody in trouble!"

"Should have thought about that before you screwed around with the FBI," Jody said with an admirable helping of her own spitefulness.

"Have a good shift, Daniels," Stan said, following Jody out of the room. "And don't even listen to any of his—" The heavy door slammed on his final words, but the meaning was clear enough. Agent Daniels stood staring after them, his mouth hanging open in shock and disbelief. His shift ended at 6:00 A.M., and by the time someone got around to hauling me in front of the higher powers—probably mid-morning—the story would have circulated throughout the building several times.

There's something addictive about the roar of the grease-paint and the smell of the crowd.

▽

22

"MIKE," THE UNNERVED young agent said in answer to my question.

"Well, Mike," I said, readjusting the cumbersome chains and trying to get comfortable against the white bars that stood between us, "did you ever do anything *really* stupid?"

Mike Daniels sat at his desk, doing everything he could think of so as not to stare. It must have been a difficult couple of days for a young, enthusiastic junior agent who had grand ideas of justice and who was anxious to serve God and country by fighting *serious* crime and corruption. First they make him lock up a fourteen-year-old boy who'd had too much to drink; then, a night later, they dump a chained-up crippled man on the floor of the same cell. To add to his discomfort, an empty black wheelchair sat accusingly near the wall to his left. Somewhere in the back of his mind, I'm sure he was wondering whether he'd really signed on with the good guys or not.

"Yeah," he said slowly. "I guess."

"Well, I've sure been a bonehead," I said, shaking my head. "Those guys were my friends before I let curiosity kill the old cat."

"How *did* you get in there?" he said, almost whispering. Stan and Jody said he would ask, and that anything I said would be compared to my official story the next day.

I told him the whole Star Spangled tale, *exactly* the way it happened, with special emphasis on my determination to save the mall rat I was convinced had been framed not once but twice.

"It was just irresistible," I concluded, "getting through a restricted door, and then unexpectedly being given the chance to save days, maybe weeks checking out a few of my suspects. Stupid, huh?"

"Well, I guess it was a pretty unique opportunity," Mike said enthusiastically. " 'The Star Spangled Banner,' huh? I never even noticed that!"

My old editor, Randy White, was a vain, neurotic, hedonistic, crusty geezer with a heart of gold. He often ranted about how it was I got him and "half the east coast of central Florida" to "adopt" me. Before Randy made a point of it, I'd never really noticed, but there was no denying that many people just seemed to trust me, seemed generally willing to go along with what Randy always called my harebrained ideas. People trusted my dad like that, but then he genuinely earned their trust, and there was nothing harebrained about him.

Mike Daniels never had a chance. He not only gave me back my chair (along with my computer) but he let me use his desk phone to dump my story to the paper. My "Stick Was a Bad Boy" column for the day would make me out to be a recalcitrant and mischievous member of the fourth estate, would make the FBI out to be faithful and diligent protectors of the common good, and would make the good people of central Florida laugh. At me. Between the lines, I was doing everything I could to create a groundswell of support for my favorite juvenile delinquent, Billy Simpson.

In the morning I felt like the juvenile delinquent, sitting in front of Stan and Jody's chief (Senior Agent Elmore Badger), retelling my story, and listening to his lecture. Fortunately, old Elmore had heard the rumors about Stan and Jody's wrath, and he'd also read my column in the morning paper. It was far more like a disappointed father speech than being read the proverbial riot act, and I was certain early on that no charges were to be filed. The old guy even gave Stan and Jody a few mild but concerned words about being overzealous.

It was a beautiful thing.

My charm ran out, however, when it came to getting any more information about Fred Lucas.

"Are you totally nuts?" Jody exclaimed, when I started pumping her on the drive back to my apartment. "You just lucked out in a big way, and now you've got the gall to try and compromise me again! Any search from my terminal traces immediately back to me."

"Jody, I'd never try to compromise you," I said, letting just a hint of hurt temper my words. "I respect you too much as a person. Besides, I'm happily married."

"In your dreams, Foster."

"Okay, look, Jody. You can't tell me anything about *who* our Fred Lucas is; but can you at least find out *what* he did? *Especially* if it was mob or drug related. Think about it, a retired drug guy, living a dull but relatively safe life at the taxpayers' expense. He gets bored, misses the action, and starts a little moonlighting operation at the local mall."

"And so he kills a little old lady? Come on, Stick. Get real."

"Okay, that doesn't fit in too well, but what if he was trying to kill Luigi Leone?"

"Why?"

"I don't know. Wait! Maybe Louie recognized him! Yes, Jody, it's perfect! A Little Italy pizza guy probably sees lots of things on the streets of New York City. The two of them happen to end up at the same mall in Florida, and bingo . . . maybe blackmail. And who knows, Fred Lucas could have been supplying the Vipers. At least check it out. . . ."

"All right," Jody said grudgingly, "I'll look into it. I'll even ask the OPD to question the Vipers about any connections with Lucas. Happy?"

"Ecstatic."

I thanked Jody for the ride, and when she brought my chair up from the trunk, I just couldn't resist being a wiseguy one more time.

"You know, Jody, your acting was wonderful; I mean, I believed you, you were so good. But, if I may be so bold, we've got to work on your walk, your body language. You're a little stiff, Jody. Maybe it's the suit or the 10mm and the shoulder holster. Maybe it's the bullet-proof bra—I don't know—but you've got to learn to loosen up a little. Try to let all that natural, sensuous beauty flow out through your arms and legs. You know, think beautiful; be beautiful. . . ."

"Shut up, chauvinist pig!"

Yes, ma'am.

Sam's note, placed symbolically over my morning's column in the newspaper, consisted simply of several pencil sketches. The first, a man in a wheelchair, was presumably me. The second was a fair representation of an automobile gas gauge with its needle all the way at the top. The last image was that of a large barnyard animal with sturdy horns and a ring in its nose.

Everybody's a critic.

After a night in chains, I reckoned that I deserved another Strawberry Delight. This time, however, I did it right, lightly toasting the iced cinnamon raisin bread until it was ever-so-golden brown and the icing was melting down the sides. The butter (like the icing, representing the dairy group) went on more smoothly this time, and by the strawberry and Cheerio layers, the warm aroma had my mouth watering. I'd worry about my beard later.

I was a sticky mess when I answered the kitchen phone. Okay, I'd worry about my beard *and* the telephone receiver later.

"Hello?" I said as clearly as the heavenly concoction in my mouth allowed.

"Stick?"

"Yeah. Billy? You okay?"

"Sure," he said stoutly, but then quickly changed his tone. "I mean, well, not really. Look, Stick, I'm trying to do like you said; you know, be honest about everything?"

"Good. And?"

"Well. Jeez, Stick, I don't like it here. I'm lonely; I mean, I miss my friends. And . . ." he trailed off and I heard him swallow hard.

"And?"

"And I'm scared. Okay? There. You happy?"

"No," I said, smiling to myself, "I won't be happy until you're out of there and bumming pizza off me again. There. You happy?"

"Better. Were you really in the FBI slammer last night?"

"You bet."

"It's a drag in there, huh?"

"Yeah, but I wasn't asleep through it all like you."

"Okay, okay. Can you come down today?"

"When?"

"The sooner the better."

"Give me half an hour."

"Thanks, Stick. I mean it."

"I know you do, Billy. Later."

After I got myself unstuck from the phone, I soaked a dishrag with hot water and cleaned up as best I could. Then, before driving down to Juvey, I toasted two more pieces of iced cinnamon raisin bread, built another Strawberry Delight, and wrapped it up in aluminum foil.

After all, kids need a well-balanced diet too.

▽

23

"It's just for a few days," I pleaded.

"A few days until what? He hates Juvey, okay, but he doesn't want to go home and he can't go back to living in the mall duct work. What's going to change in a few days?"

"I don't know, Sam. But they'll let him out if we'll just take him in. Maybe I can talk him into going home and learning to tolerate his mother."

"Sure. And you can teach him to fly while you're at it. I knew you'd end up adopting one of those dead-end kids, Stick; you're such a sucker. But *that* one? Couldn't it be any of them but that one? What about Emily? I'll even talk 'girl stuff' with her. I promise."

"Sam, come on. Billy needs help. Now. Help from somebody who believes in him. Maybe that's all the difference it takes for a kid like Billy . . . someone who cares, and someone who believes he can be somebody."

"Now you sound like Jesse Jackson."

"So?"

"One week. Not a day more."

I have a dream. . . .

There was something strangely cathartic about having the mall rats all together again for lunch the next day . . . especially since Sam's money was paying for their pizza.

They asked Billy all about his adventures at the Federal Building and the Orange County Juvenile Detention Center. He struggled, but I had to hand it to him; he answered their questions carefully and honestly, looking at me and checking himself each time the urge to embellish or brag threatened to overcome him.

I used Louie's phone to call Constance Galliger and set up a beach day for Friday. I got the distinct feeling that she'd been hoping I'd forget. Then I made another appointment with the smiling pizza man for later that same afternoon. Somehow I was pretty sure the smile wouldn't last when I started asking him about Fred Lucas. It was either the FBI or me, and I figured that I had a considerably better chance of getting some kind of an answer. But then, I'd been wrong before.

When they were caught up on Billy, it was my turn.

"So, Rollin' Homeboy," Wallace said with a grin, "you know you always been sort of a *roll* model for us. . . . I crack myself up!"

Uh-oh.

"You're the kinda guy we all wannabe, Stick Monster," Danny added earnestly.

"Well, like, except Tam and me," Emily said with a wink. "But you know what Danny means."

"And," Wallace went on soberly, "now we hear you broke into the FBI building and got busted."

"We've been thinking about ways to emulate your recent behavior," Jeremy said.

Everyone laughed when I rolled my eyes.

"Well," Tamara said softly, "to be honest, the Geek had to tell us what 'emulate' was, but then we went right to work on it!"

"And," Jeremy continued smoothly, "I believe that we have put together an impressive top-ten list of federal offenses to which we might aspire. Danny?"

After Rocketeering and Circumcision (tampering with the U.S. Male), I didn't hear much of Danny Singer's napkin-long list. I was laughing too hard. The kids had me right where they wanted me, and they weren't about to let up. It was wonderful to see them enjoy giving me a well-deserved but good-natured ribbing. Billy seemed especially pleased, and each time I glanced at him, he held his palm to his nose to indicate how severely I was being "faced."

Dead-end kids, huh? What does Sam know about kids anyway?

"Just what are you getting at?" Louie asked, firmly interrupting my not-so-graceful beating around the proverbial bush.

"Look, Louie," I said, still wavering about how to proceed, "I really need to know if you ever knew or even saw Fred Lucas *before* you opened your shop here. Like in New York maybe?"

"Why?" The tone of his voice and the look in his dark eyes told me that I'd get nothing without full disclosure. The rising cigarette smoke suddenly seemed to cast his face in an ominous light.

"It's just a wild theory." I was hemming and hawing again. "I mean, could Fred Lucas have had a reason to want you dead?"

"The clothing salesman?" Louie's suspicion turned to incredulity, almost humor. "I've never purchased anything from him, but I doubt he would assassinate me for that!"

"You didn't answer my first question, Louie. Did you ever see the guy before you moved down here?"

"Well," he answered, all signs of tension gone from his voice and his face, "it's funny you should ask. I thought about that once myself, long ago. You know how it is; sometimes everybody looks like someone else. But I don't think I ever came to any real conclusion. Until you just asked, I'd forgotten all about it."

"Did you say anything to him about it?"

"No, I don't think so."

"Did you mention it to anyone else, or talk about it where someone might overhear?"

"I don't really remember, but it wouldn't surprise me if the thought came to me while I was working. I think out loud all the time," Louie said, a smile spreading across his face. "My sons have asked me to stop. It embarrasses them!"

"So that means *if* you said something about *maybe* knowing him out loud, Fred Lucas *could* have heard about it around the mall?"

"I suppose so, but what would it mat—" Louie's quick eyes lit up as understanding spread steadily across his face. "Fred Lucas isn't Fred Lucas, is he?"

"No, Louie, he isn't."

"Well, well. Fred and I will have to have a little talk. We can't have the poor guy worrying his secret life away!"

"I'm afraid that's not possible. He's been moved away . . . rather suddenly."

"Why?"

"Well, that's where things got a little out of hand. I sort of let on that I knew, and tried to get some information out of him. That's when he spooked, and the spooks moved him out."

"Stick," Louie said firmly, "this is where I want you to assure me that before you scared our salesman friend away, you convinced him that I wasn't the one who tipped you off."

Oops.

"Not tonight."

Her tone of voice left no room for debate. I never realized that two words could carry so many pointed interpretations. As thick as I can be sometimes when it comes to male-female matters, even I didn't need to be told that Sam had also said: "As long as *he* is out there on the living room sofa, *you* might as well be out there too." Somehow implicit in the words was the obvious and irrefutable truth that this turn of events had clearly been my doing, and that I alone bore responsibility for my present dilemma.

My dad used to read through the *Living Proverbs* once every month. He began each day by reading the chapter that corresponded with the calender date. For some reason he always quoted more often from the twelfth to the twentieth of each month, and one of his favorite nuggets was: "Kindness makes a man more attractive." If memory serves, that little bit of wisdom came from chapter nineteen. All I had to do now was figure out the relationship between my being attractive, and my being in the proverbial doghouse.

▽

24

CONSTANCE GALLIGER'S LITTLE beach on Fish Lake wasn't Daytona or New Smyrna, not by a long shot. There would be no family sedans carrying sun worshippers up and down this stretch of Florida shoreline. When she said that her father had trucked in sand, she wasn't kidding; it was pure white silica and must have been over a foot deep.

The winding path from the house to the beach was bad enough, almost 50 yards of grove sand, scrub oak, and palmetto bushes. The mall rats were struggling before we ever reached the *real* sand, and started working in shifts to haul my chair to the water. When they hit the beach and my wheels *really* dug in, burying themselves well past the handrims, they almost left me there to fend for myself.

"Hey, Rollin' Homeboy," Wallace complained, stopping to wipe the sweat from his face, "you been puttin' on some weight, or what? I think we oughta get overtime for this."

"And I thought you guys were tough."

As he stepped up and took hold of my chair's aluminum alloy frame, Jeremy said: "Once more into the beach, dear friends, once more!" with a flourish worthy of Henry V. Of course, it seemed to me that he had avoided his turn several times by waiting for Tamara to step in ahead of him.

" 'Be he ne'er so vile,' " he continued, as he stumbled through the deep sand, struggling to keep up with his stronger friends, " 'this day shall gentle his condition. And gentlemen in England now abed shall think themselves accursed they were not here, and hold their manhood cheap while any speaks that fought with us upon' Stick Man's Day!"

Okay, so I was impressed.

They all seemed a little surprised when, after they finally wrestled my wheelchair to the water's edge, I pulled off my shirt and loafers and hopped out onto the sand.

"Ouch!" I said involuntarily when my palms hit the sandy deck. "It's a bit toasty." Fortunately, I couldn't feel the effect the hot sand was having on my bare legs as I dragged my cutoffs into the cool water. "Ahhh!"

They just stood watching, apparently waiting to see how long it would be before they had to rescue me.

"Relax, guys. I don't kick so good anymore, but I can still outswim you wimps!"

I reclined in the water and showed off my backstroke. "Come on in," I called as I quickly left them behind. "The water's great!"

Within seconds, they were splashing and thrashing, fighting over the two inner tubes, and generally having a wonderful time. I was a bit embarrassed by the size—or rather, lack thereof—of Emily's bathing suit, but none of the other guys seemed to mind, so I kept my objections to myself. After twenty minutes or so, Wallace offered me his turn with one of the inner tubes in exchange for the use of the collapsible spinning rig I had retrieved from my Monte Carlo's trunk.

"Deal," I said.

The Galliger estate had no dock, but the neighbor fifty or seventy-five yards down the beach to the west did. When Wallace asked me if he could fish from it, I told him I was the wrong one to ask and backstroked the inner tube farther out into the lake. He rolled his eyes but trudged off down the beach, disappearing into the scrub oak for several minutes before reappearing with a high sign and taking up a casting position out over the water.

The lake was small by most standards, maybe three-quarters of a mile across. It had five other homes on it that I could see. Constance Galliger's home, the largest and the oldest, was partially hidden by oak trees draped in Spanish moss, and clearly looked the eeriest. It reminded me of a television show I'd seen once; perhaps it was a "Twilight Zone." All I could remember was a foggy southern dirt road, swathed in Spanish moss, with a long line of Civil War veterans marching wearily along it. They all turned out to be ghosts, as I recall. The Galliger home would have fit right in.

Like the OPD, I'd never really considered Constance Galliger a very likely suspect; even now, knowing something about her rebellious teenage years, the idea was pretty silly. Still, if she'd appeared at that moment, glowering out at me from an upper story window, I could have been persuaded to reevaluate her status. Instead of anything so sinister, she came out the screened kitchen door and headed down the path with a large wooden tray. Needless to say, the lemonade and cookies were a great hit and, unless I was losing my sense of people, she was actually enjoying the kids' exuberant gratitude.

As I made my way back to shore, Tamara waded out to me with a jelly-jar glass and a Toll House cookie.

"Thank you, Tamara."

"You're welcome," she said, almost whispering. "You know, Miss Galliger's not so bad, is she?"

"I wouldn't think so," I whispered back with a wink. She laughed and pushed my tube out toward deeper water before splashing her way back onto the beach. I managed to keep my cookie dry but spilled lemonade all over my stomach.

I was watching Constance trudge back to the old house when Wallace called out from the neighbor's dock. It sounded like he said, "The dog has died."

"What? What dog died?" I shouted back across the water. Several others were also yelling the same kind of questions at him.

He held my spinning rod in his armpit, cupped his hands around his mouth, and tried again.

"Look! The dog has eyes!"

The dog has eyes? It was still nonsense, but we all turned to look as he pointed out toward the middle of Fish Lake with my pole. There was, not a "dog," but a *log*, floating maybe 60 or 80 yards out. I was much closer to it than anyone else, but I didn't understand about the eyes part . . . until they blinked, and the log disappeared beneath the surface.

"Hurry, Stick!" Emily shouted.

"Stroke! Stroke! Stroke!" Jeremy yelled through his own cupped hands. (They told me later that he was easily the first one out of the water.)

"Come on, Stickster!" Danny said, grabbing the tube and hauling me the rest of the way up to the beach. "I ain't hangin' around here all day waiting for ya ta be gator bait!"

"Grab him," Billy instructed the others, and before I could say a word, they threw me in my chair and started hauling me backward, away from the water's edge . . . considerably faster than we had come.

Wallace caught up with us at the edge of the woods.

"I been watchin' it float across the lake for half an hour," he said between heavy intakes of breath. "Even when I teased you guys about the bumps on it, until it went under, I thought it *was* a log."

"Stop! Stop here," I said. "Let's see where it comes up."

"The American species of the alligator," Jeremy said, edging closer to the house, "can stay underwater for over an hour and has been filmed jumping five vertical feet to snatch prey off an overhanging limb. I think we should keep going."

"Look!" Billy said, pointing to the exact spot where I had been floating, sunning, and sipping lemonade only a moment before. The alligator broke the surface with a vengeance. "He's an aggressive little guy, isn't he?"

"The American alligator," Jeremy went on insistently, "unlike its Chinese cousin, can reach lengths of twenty feet."

"Chill, Geek," Emily said, backhanding him, but keeping her eyes on the hungry-looking beast.

"He's watching us," Tamara said.

"Yeah," Wallace said in a low voice, "like a shopper cruising the meat counter at the store. I think he likes you, Tam!"

"Cut it out!" She moved closer to Jeremy.

"It sure looks that way," I said as the sun sank into the

trees across the lake to our left. With another blink, the great creature sank out of sight.

"The American alligator," Jeremy said, grabbing the back of my chair and tugging uselessly, "when hunting on land, can for brief stretches reach speeds of nearly forty miles per hour. They have, on occasion, been known to catch horses."

Nothing more needed saying. One second I was sitting under the eaves of Miss Constance's oaks and the next I was flying backward up the path toward her kitchen door. The mall rats were screaming like banshees. Before I could get them settled down, our hostess stomped past us, scanning the jungle with the business end of a double-barreled 12-gauge shotgun.

The very sight of her, stalking the path like the Terminator, was enough to silence the kids.

"Where is it?" she said, looking back at us with death in her eyes.

"Jeez! There!" Danny screamed, pointing back to where twelve feet of alligator was lumbering up onto the sand. "Shoot it! Shoot it!"

Constance Galliger let the shotgun down with a look of disgust, and started back toward us. "You children should be more thoughtful. You had me all worried for nothing," she said as she past us on her way back to the house.

The hungry log was still trudging determinedly in our direction, and the mall rats all fell in step behind the woman with the gun.

"Guys! Hey, guys! Remember me?"

"Whoa! Sorry, Homey," Wallace said, rushing back with the others to get me.

"I think she's nuts," Danny whispered in my ear.

"It's still coming," Jeremy said. None of us had taken our eyes off the creature slogging up the beach toward us.

"I thought you'd seen a coral snake," Constance said, disappearing into the kitchen. The door slammed closed behind her, but her voice carried through the screen. "I *hate* coral snakes."

We were piling into the shiny new Oldsmobile next to the house when Constance reappeared, carrying what looked for all the world like a small rump roast. We stared in silent amazement as she strolled down the path, paused near the edge of the sand, and tossed the raw meat to the approaching gator with a clean, practiced underhand.

We waited in what we all hoped was the relative safety of the car as Constance returned up the path and walked over to where we sat cowering with the windows rolled mostly up. She was slightly winded when she arrived, and with a last glance toward the beach, I let down the window all the way, as she clearly had something to say.

"I probably should have told you about Rufuss."

"Ouch! Not tonight."

"I said I was sorry about Billy."

"It's not that."

"Well, what is it then?"

"It's this awful sunburn I got at Constance Galliger's today. Ouch! Oh, okay, if you *must*. Just be careful about—"

Mmmm . . .

▽

25

I WAS PRETTY uncomfortable in church on Sunday, and I didn't feel any better on Monday morning; in fact, it was clear that I was only beginning to feel bad. Lying on that inner tube for almost two hours was not unlike being tuna salad on an English muffin under the oven's broiler element, only the tuna salad can't splash water on itself. It knows perfectly well that it's being cooked. And, as far as I know, tuna doesn't peel three days later.

"Hello?" answered the deep voice in my car phone's earpiece.

"Hi, Stet. It's me."

"You! Stick, how *could* you? I sold you that beautiful classic because I thought it meant something to you, because I thought you would take care of it. I drove by the body shop the other day . . . made me cry."

"It's not like there was anything I could do, Stet."

"If you'd just buy a gun," the Orlando Orange Wheels player-coach said, not for the first time. "It's not like you can't handle one."

"Yeah, well, I shot enough people last year to do me for a lifetime, thank you. Besides, I'm a writer, not a fighter."

"The way you write sometimes, you'd better buy the gun."

"Funny. Look, does your route today take you anywhere near the Palmetto Plaza food court? I'm buying."

"Sure. How about three o'clock?"

"Great. Thanks, Stet. I've got a few questions, and I want you to meet my mall rats."

"Sam told me you were turning into Father Flanigan!" he said with a laugh. "See ya there."

I dialed again while I headed west through town on Colonial Drive. Out where nearly everything is newly developed along the main east-west thoroughfare—almost out to White Road and the Galliger Gator Farm—there's a shady shopping plaza on the south side of the highway. An old high school friend runs a cozy shop called Little Oak Books. Well, we had once been friends, anyway. There were many reasons why I should have called her when I first moved back to Orlando, but there were just enough others that I had not been able to do so.

"Ellie? It's Nick Foster."

The breathing was barely audible on the other end; in fact, it might only have been line noise. I mentally kicked myself for calling. *Bad move, Stick.*

"I'm sorry, Ellie," is what I said out loud. "This was a bad idea; I'll let you go."

"No! Where are you?"

"I'm on my way out."

"Come. I'll meet you out front."

"Well, actually, I've never seen your new shop. Everyone says it's wonderful."

"No!"

"Okay. Sorry."

Sorry summed up my troubled thoughts when it came to Ellie. Eleanor Algretto was my first love. It was, at the time, an almost perfect friendship between classmates that grew into going steady almost immediately after her previous boyfriend, David Peterson, went off to college.

As a freshman, I played football with David, a tall, lanky tight end with an easy smile and a gentle manner. I was nearly as tall, but David had twenty pounds of solid muscle on me. He never talked about Ellie the way other seniors often talked about their dates. I respected him for that. As a second-string defensive end on the varsity squad, I went head to head with David every day in practice, and unlike the other seniors—the entire offensive backfield—he never felt the need to crush me into oblivion. He moved me out of his way with easy efficiency, often taking me aside afterward to pass on helpful tips.

Then, a year later, thanks in part to David's coaching (the fifteen new pounds and the weight training didn't hurt either), I had David's place on the varsity team. And, strangely enough, I had David's girl too. They had mutually agreed on the separation, Ellie had assured me. She'd always been the perfect friend, so easy and comfortable to be around. We'd always laughed and talked in a way that was unusual with adolescent boys and girls. Maybe it was the freedom from sexual tension; what freshman in his right mind would consider putting the moves on a senior's girl?

But falling in love didn't change that part of our relationship at all. There was no need to try to *make* conversation while what I was really thinking about was kissing her wonderfully soft lips. Conversation still came naturally . . . even though her lips often made me forget what we had been talking about. For that year we were the school couple. We turned heads at every dance and dined in some of Orlando's finest restaurants.

My part-time job at the sporting goods store barely kept gas in the car and paid for movie tickets, but Ellie's dad had this thing about his daughter eating in primo places. Oh, we still hit Burger Man occasionally, but more often than not, Mr. Algretto slipped me forty bucks and instructed me to "take Eleanor someplace nice for dinner."

Yes, sir!

When summer came, we traveled farther afield, spending our dates at the races in Daytona, on the rides at Busch Gardens, or at the Volusia County Fair. Looking back, I realize now that I was just not prepared, sexually, to go anywhere near as far as Ellie was probably willing to go. She didn't exactly push herself on me, but the passion in her embraces often left me bewildered (and sweating), caught between what I had been taught about the real meaning of sexual intimacy by my father, and what my recently awakened body wanted more than anything in the world. The longer and longer drives to and from our dates left less and less time in which to be tempted.

That inner debate ended suddenly. We'd just arrived back at her house after a rather subdued summer afternoon and evening at the Volusia County Fair. Ellie was the one who got me to add country music to my already eclectic musical preferences, and the Oak Ridge Boys were one of her all-time favorite groups. Their concert that night at the fairgrounds was outstanding and the crowd really got into it, but I couldn't get Ellie to dance with me in the aisles. Something was wrong, but as is unfortunately my penchant, I couldn't have seen it coming if five trained bird dogs stood pointing their noses in the right direction.

"I have something to tell you," Ellie said, taking both my hands as we stood by the back door to her palatial Windemere home. "I think I've made a mistake, done something I should have talked about with you first."

At least I could be sure she wasn't pregnant, I remember thinking with some chagrin at the time.

"David's been calling me, begging me to see him, to talk to him in person."

Or could I?

"I finally agreed, and went out with him last night . . . just to tell him that it was really over, and that I was in love with you."

I didn't even allow myself to hear the last part of her admission. The first part so totally and unexpectedly shattered my fragile sixteen-year-old male ego, that I just dropped her hands and walked away. Forever.

Of all the deplorable things I've done in my life, that was probably the worst. Of course I didn't know it then; it took me years to grow up and figure it out. Trashing the dating relationship was stupid beyond all reason; throwing away the friendship was unforgivable.

"Hi, Ellie," I said, throwing open the Oldsmobile's passenger door. "Burger Man okay?"

"Burger Man is fine," she said, getting in and fastening her seat belt.

I stared past her, at the window display of her book shop. "It's really great, Ellie. You've done a beautiful job." I meant the words; they came straight from my heart. But they sounded hollow to me.

The car door closed, and when my passenger turned her brown eyes on me, I almost stopped breathing. After all those years Ellie still wore the same perfume, a fragrance I can't make myself forget. I never asked what it was, but to this day, I turn around in a crowd and look for her when I smell it on someone else. The effects were still the same. I struggled not to stare at the soft curves of her lips while memories of youth came rushing back. This was going to be even harder than I had thought.

Bad move, Stick.

"You're sunburned. Let's get out of here."

Yes, ma'am.

▽

26

WE DIDN'T SPEAK again until the static-enhanced voice behind Burger Man's rotund plastic smile asked us what we wanted.

"Two Cheese Man Specials, two fries, one cola, one lemon-lime," I said without thinking. Shocked at my own continued stupidity, I turned to find that Ellie was smiling.

"You remember."

"Sorry. I wasn't thinking; I should have asked."

"It's exactly what I wanted."

We parked in the shade under a beautifully spreading oak tree in the West Orlando Cemetery, the same place I left my old Z-28 Camaro during Jim Woods's burial service a year before.

"Why here?" Ellie asked.

"It's shady. And a kindred spirit I never met is buried right over there," I said, pointing across the hardy Bahia grass.

"Of course," she said. "Jim Woods. I followed that story every day. Pretty exciting stuff."

We ate in silence for a time. I felt more and more uncomfortable, not because Ellie was doing anything to make it so, but because there are some ghosts that insist on tricking us by treating us to unattractive memories of ourselves. I sat there, staring out at Jim Woods's gravestone and remembering vivid pictures of high school parties and dances, the junior and senior proms, and game trips where the cheerleaders shared the bus with the basketball and football teams. Ellie was in every memory; silent, sad, and totally void of any bitterness or anger.

When, during the first half of our junior year, Ellie turned down all date offers (they came from nearly every guy in the school), I pretended not to notice. It would pass, I was sure. But she waited. For the next two years Ellie waited; quietly, patiently, and without an unkind word. I blocked it all out, building a wall around my life. Self-defense is such a noble endeavor in principle, but when used by a blockheaded adolescent to justify hurting a friend, it is an especially heinous act of violence.

"I was a real jerk, El."

"I know."

"I'm really sorry."

"So you've said, and I forgave you . . . remember?"

"Yeah, but it will never feel any better, will it?"

"Life goes on. What did you want to see me about?"

"It's the Galliger murder. I'm running down what few leads I have. One of them—albeit a flimsy one—is the Citrus Growers Association."

"Ah. You want Daddy, not me. I should have known you weren't ready yet."

"El, that's not funny," I said, feeling a strange chill at the words "ready yet."

"You're right. But why didn't you just call him?"

"Are you kidding?"

"Ah, Nick the Naive. Did you think Daddy blamed you for what happened between us?"

"Of course. It was my fault."

"Maybe. But you were going to be the son he never had, Nick. The first and only boy I ever dated that he trusted. David was 'too old,' and all the others 'only wanted one thing.' You walked on water, love . . . and I drove you away. 'Eleanor,' he said a hundred times, 'that Foster boy is honorable, like his father. He wouldn't know an ulterior motive if it hit him from behind.' "

"I didn't know."

"Then you're the only one who didn't. Everyone in my family—from grandparents to third and fourth cousins—knows about the one Eleanor let get away."

"I'm sorry."

"I know, and that's a start. What do you want with the CGA?"

"Well," I said, feeling more unsettled than ever but determined to finish what I had started, "Constance Galliger says that Martha wasn't very popular in the organization. She's sure no one would kill her sister over it, but I'd like to know more about just how unpopular she was. I thought you might get your dad to shed some light on that little circle, particularly how they felt about Martha."

"Did I ever tell you what Daddy was going to give us for the junior prom?"

"No," I said, cringing, "what?"

"A limo ride and dinner at the Citrus Club."

The Citrus Club, atop one of downtown's tallest office buildings, was Orlando's most exclusive restaurant. Members only; though while in high school, I had no idea what kind of members that meant.

"Is it true that there are no prices on the menu?"

"Of course."

Mm.

"Will you talk to your dad?" I said, cranking up the Cutlass and absentmindedly pushing the cassette back into the Delco tape deck.

"Of course, I will," Ellie said. Then she laughed out loud, but tears also formed in the corners of her eyes. "We were made for each other, Nick. The first time I ever heard her, I knew you'd love K. T. Oslin."

While I drove back to the book shop, K. T. and Ellie sang "Eighties Ladies." I just fought my nervous stomach and the knot in my throat.

After high school—and after hiding in the army for two years, pretending to grow up—I went off to college, met what I thought was a wonderful young lady, and finally decided that maybe girls were okay after all. A year later, I even thought that marriage might be a pretty good deal, so I bought a ring, she accepted, and everything looked like it was working out just fine. That summer, however, I fell off the garage roof. Instead of coming down to cheer me on and reaffirm her love, my wonderful fiancée placed several polite get-well calls to Florida Hospital before mailing back my ring with a poorly written "Dear Gimp" letter.

Unfortunately, that was the same day Ellie found out about my spinal injury and came to the hospital for what must surely have been a selfless show of friendship and moral support. I didn't hear a word she said that evening. I wasn't listening to anyone, just blocking everything and everybody out. All I remembered in the years afterwards were the tears in her eyes as she walked away. Needless to say, Ellie didn't visit me again . . . but her cards arrived every week.

"Thanks, El," I said, pulling up to the curb in front of Little Oak Books. "Next time can I see your shop?"

"No."

"Okay, sorry."

"Stop saying that. I'll call you after I talk to Daddy Warbucks," she said, climbing out of the car and leaning back in to look squarely at my sunburned face. Her earth-tone print sundress hung open in the front, revealing far more than I needed to see . . . the stuff of ancient dreams. "It was good to see you, Nick."

Yeah. Good like a kick in the teeth.

"I thought about sending you an invitation to the wedding, El," I said lamely, "but it seemed crass somehow. Like most things between you and me, I just didn't know how to handle it, so I left it alone."

"It's okay," she said with a wry smile that I hadn't seen in many years, "I went anyway." She winked, shut the car door, and disappeared into her bookshop.

You *what?*

I was still a wreck when I arrived at the Palmetto Plaza food court to wait for Joe Stetler. Listening on the way to K. T. Oslin sing "Wall of Tears" and "Do You Still Love Me?" hadn't helped me lighten up much, but life is hard all over.

Fortunately, the mall rats had come and gone; they were probably at the video arcade. I sat by my window, stared at the crowded parking lot below, and wondered why people things had to be so complicated. I like to think of myself as a basically nice guy, but don't we all? For as long as I lived, Eleanor Algretto would be a gut-wrenching reminder of what a nice guy can do.

As hard as that emotional baggage is to deal with, I was, at that moment, nearly as troubled by Ellie's parting words. How could Eleanor have been at my wedding without my noticing? She certainly didn't pass through the reception line. Hats. There were a number of hats in the brightly colored crowd. She must have been wearing a hat. And why . . .

"Hello, Mr. Stick. I bought this for you."

Charlie Martin handed me what was surely a vanilla cola, my favorite afternoon drink. His smile, so warm and real, burned through me like a forest fire through a dry palmetto stand. My throat constricted as I reached for my backpack and my wallet.

"No," he said, patting me on the shoulder with one hand while he waved the other. "It's my treat!"

Then the tears came. Why couldn't I have been just a little bit more like Charlie Martin?

"Thank you, Charlie," I said, wiping my face and smiling through my embarrassment, "for this, and for being my friend."

The young cleanup man nodded knowingly. "You were my friend first," he said, and with a look at his watch and a parting pat on my back, he went cheerfully back to work, quietly singing the Traveling Wilburys tune I had taught him: "Going to the End of the Line."

And the people said . . . Amen.

▽

27

"WHO RAN OVER your dog?"

"Hi, Stet. Oh, I just had a little visit from the Ghost of Christmas Past," I said, knowing there was no point in pretending. "Darned inconsiderate of him, dropping by to scare me in July, but there you are."

" 'Wherever you go,' " Stet said with a gentle laugh, " 'there you are.' "

"YoYoDyne Industries, wasn't it?" I said, a smile coming more easily. " 'Where the future begins tomorrow.' "

"Yeah, that was it," Stet agreed. " 'Monkey boys in the facility! There are monkey boys in the facility!' "

We laughed together while Stet pushed a mall chair out of his way and rolled up to my table. The Orlando Orange Wheels' last all-night rental movie marathon was a collection of the bizarre. We watched *Yellowbeard,* all twelve episodes of "Fawlty Towers," and a Doc Savage spoof called *Buckaroo Banzai: Adventures in the Eighth Dimension.* Before he was RoboCop, Peter Weller starred with John Lithgow in this sci-fi send-up filled with useless but memorable quotes.

"You okay?"

"Better," I said. "Thanks. My kids are off somewhere—probably protecting the galaxy one token at a time—but I wanted to ask you about the Green Berets. Didn't you say you thought about that gig once?"

"Only for a second or two. Okay, so I was a first lieutenant, but I'm really smarter than that implies. What'd you wanna know?"

"Well, besides the additional training, what kind of security stuff's involved with being a Green Beanie? I mean, did I read somewhere that they all have some kind of secret clearance?"

"*Top* Secret clearance," Stet said. "Those guys sometimes work directly for the CIA; you know, all those places we never went and all those things we never did? Well, the Green Berets are the guys who never went, and didn't do anything while they weren't there."

"How would I check out an ex-beret's security file? Who has access to those kind of records?"

"You got a Pentagon colonel in your pocket somewhere, Stick? I didn't think so. Even your FBI buddies'd get the cold shoulder if they tried to snoop into a Beanie's background. I mean his Form Two-fourteen might not be hard to get at. Even with two years, *Private* Foster, you've got one of those. It tells where you took basic, where you were stationed, what training you got, any awards, honors, et cetera, but the kind of file you're talking about is buried deep."

"Gotcha. So, do these guys specialize in one area, or do they learn a lot about everything?"

"Both. I think there are eleven guys on a typical team. Each one will have specialized in maybe two or three areas—you know, communications, engineering, demolition, light weapons, medical, whatever, but they also learn enough so that they can cover for each other in a pinch."

"How likely is it, do you think, that a Green Beret would come out of the army and put all that training—say, in engineering—to use as a janitor?"

"Not likely but not impossible either. A guy like that would be capable of designing and building, or blowing up, just about anything. He could make big bucks almost anywhere, I'd think, but then maybe this guy just had enough of the pressure and the bureaucracy and wanted to do his own thing, at his own pace. Who are we talkin' about here anyway?"

"The head maintenance guy at this mall."

"The wimpy little white guy whose pants are always falling down?"

"Yup."

"The guy who saved your butt the other night?"

"The very same."

"Well, you just never know, do you?"

Not by a long shot.

Okay, so there was lots more to Fred Lucas and Ernest Boyle than met one's eye. In both cases, it was the motive that failed to satisfy. Would Fred Lucas kill Luigi Leone to protect his identity? It seemed unlikely. As evidenced by Fred's hasty and all-expenses-paid move, Uncle Sam was apparently more than willing to oblige him should he feel threatened. Surely the salesclerk position at Jacob's didn't represent a life-fulfilling career track. A high-dollar drug business, however, just might.

When it came to Ernest Boyle, I had only one shaky theory. Someone (maybe even Fred Lucas) could have hired him to kill Louie; or, for that matter, Martha Galliger might have been the target all along. Still, the idea that the maintenance man was a hit man for hire was pretty hard to swallow, but stranger things have been known to happen. In any case, I needed more information about both men . . . something no one was going to give me willingly.

All of my semideductive reasoning shed no light whatsoever on the death of Leonard Gordon, which, if it had anything at all to do with the other murder, left me totally in the dark as to what that connection might be. While Billy Simpson seemed like a poor suspect in Martha's case, he was still the odds-on favorite when it came to the late mall security chief. I clearly needed some help from a pro.

"Sam said not to be late for dinner."

The familiar voice behind me, that of my mall rat house guest, had a ring of urgency to it; this from a boy who seldom went home at all. The obvious attachment Billy was forming to Sam and me was going to make getting him to reconcile with his mother even more difficult. Still, considering the alternative, we would have to face that school crossing when we came to it.

"How can we be late for dinner when it's our turn to cook it?"

"What do you mean, '*our* turn'?"

"Well, Bill, it's men's night at the Foster house. We get Mondays, Wednesdays, and Fridays. You really have to take sides on this gender thing, bud. Straddling the fence about whether you're a guy or a girl isn't good for your psyche, so either you cook with me tonight, or you cook with Sam tomorrow."

"Well, jeez! Of course I'm a guy, but I don't know anything about cooking, except some microwave stuff. Wait! Can we have those Strawberry Delight things? I think I could make one of those!"

"Nope. With men's night there's far too much at stake to wimp out with something like that. Sam and I both fancy ourselves as pretty good cooks, so it's kind of a competition thing. Some of the best chefs in the world are men; our honor is on the line tonight."

Watching young people ponder new challenges is sometimes better than watching a good stand-up comedian make faces. Kids don't always see the bigger picture, and sometimes each new experience is met with far more gravity than it actually deserves. Billy's generation has carpe diem down pat, so long as they only have to seize one moment of each day at a time. His brow furrowed in doubt and apprehension as we headed to the grocery store, and he remained in deep thought while I called the coast on my car phone.

"Hi, Butch? Stick Foster. You got a minute?"

"Sure, Stick. How's it going? I heard about the Monte. Sorry."

"Everything's okay, and the SS will be good as new in a couple of weeks. I called because I want to apply for a job, Butch. Does Delta Force Exterminators have any openings?"

When Brenda Grady isn't tending bar, she's a modern-day Jim Rockford. (And her private investigation business had nearly tripled in the year since our NASA murder and sabotage adventure drew so much media coverage.) Among her various business cards is one that says DELTA FORCE EXTERMINATORS. WE SEARCH AND DESTROY. She even has a uniform, a pump-up sprayer with dangerous-looking "Poison" stickers on it, and a couple of magnetic signs that stick to the doors of her Chevy Blazer when she's in character.

"I usually work alone," Butch said with a chuckle, "but I'm not opposed to hiring the handicapped . . . you'd probably be fun to watch! Who's getting the free critter treatment?"

"I'll tell you when you get here."

"All right, but I have to know the building address."

I told her. "How soon can you come?"

"Tomorrow morning okay?"

"Sure. Come by the apartment for me, and be sure to have the whole show going . . . signs and everything."

"You bet. What size shirt do you wear? Large?"

"Large-tall if you can get it. Thanks, Butch. Oh, and say hi to Todd for me and tell him he'll probably be getting a call from Peter. I have a job for them too."

I called Peter Stilles next.

"How's the luxury yacht, Peter?"

"Coming along nicely, thank you," he said with mock affront. "When are you coming over for a cruise?"

"Well, Peter, buddy, you know I'd just love to get out there on the Atlantic with you—maybe do the Bermuda triangle thing—but my schedule's been so hectic lately."

"Wimp."

"Fair enough. Look, Peter, I need a little computer hacking done, and was hoping that between you and Todd, I might scrounge up access to a guy's military file. What do you think?"

Before moving to Florida and taking over his late brother's blue crab fishing business, Peter was an archivist for IBM in upstate New York. He and *Melbourne Suncoaster* reporter Todd Gulick both loved to tinker with their computer modems and had between them amassed a formidable inventory of phone numbers that afforded them seemingly unrestricted access to data bases, computer networks, and research facilities that most of the rest of us never knew existed.

"We can try," he said. "Who's the guy?"

"His name's Ernest Boyle. I think his middle initial is *P*. He was a Green Beret, late 'Nam years. One of his specialties was probably engineering. I need anything you can get on him, but be careful. Joe Stetler says these guys have Top Secret clearance, and their serious files are buried at the Pentagon."

"Well, you're not asking much, are you?"

"I don't really expect you to get that, Peter, but Stet says the guy's Form Two-fourteen might not be too hard to run down. Just do what you can, okay?"

"Will do, Stick. By the way, how's the new marriage going?"

"A little tense at the moment," I said, glancing at Billy, trying to sound lighthearted. "Nothing that won't pass. Get back to me as soon as you can."

After a whirlwind tour of the local Publix, Billy and I arrived home laden with everything the aspiring gourmet chef could want. There would be a fresh fruit salad of strawberries, banana, pineapple, melon, grapes, and apples, all bathed in frozen orange juice concentrate. (Billy was positively delighted to discover not only a dish that he could prepare himself but one that required lots of knife work.)

The entree would be a lean London broil basted with Wishbone Italian Dressing and served smothered in lightly butter-sautéed mushrooms and onions. I usually liked to marinate the meat in the dressing for a day beforehand, but I'd been too preoccupied to think that far ahead. The meat would be accompanied by fresh green beans baked in a light cream sauce and covered with dried onions.

There was French bread fresh from the bakery, of course, and, for the final touch, an old family classic: Grape Dessert. One glass baking dish, one layer crushed graham crackers, one (thick) layer Breyers vanilla ice cream, one layer frozen grape juice concentrate, topped with a final layer of crushed graham crackers. Freeze until served. My mouth was already watering when I opened the apartment door.

Sam sat there at the kitchen table, pretending to read a law journal. I'm not saying she was upset, mind you, but it was definitely a little more difficult than usual, pushing the door open against all the tension. Billy must have sensed it too; he stopped just inside the door and sort of hid behind the two grocery sacks in his arms. I was trying to think of an ice breaker, but Sam beat me to it.

"Who's Ellie Algretto? And why is she calling you?"

Oops.

▽

28

I POSTPONED THE answer until after dinner, but even the exquisite meal prepared by Messrs Simpson and Foster could not altogether erase the tension. But it was close. Billy worked his tattered denim butt off, really getting into the role of international chef. His fruit salad was a work of art, and he let us both know it several times. As soon as he understood the Grape Dessert concept, he shooed me back to the main course and claimed the high-calorie creation as his own. His enthusiasm was heartening, but then I hadn't yet told him that men's night meant we did the cleanup too.

He took it pretty well, whining only briefly before realizing it wasn't going to do any good. For a time—after Sam retired to the bedroom and while the dishwasher hummed its sloshy tune—Billy and I worked side by side, silently hand washing and drying the various kitchen implements that we couldn't force into the small machine.

"It's not as bad as it seems," Billy said suddenly.

"What?"

"Sam. You know, it's probably just her period."

"Really?"

"Sure. All girls get this way once a month. She'll get over it."

"Well, thanks, Billy. That's a reassuring thing to know."

"No sweat, Stick. But who's this babe Ellie? You're not fooling around or anything, are you?"

"No, Bill, Ellie's an old high school friend, and I'm not fooling around."

"Good."

"You were a total jerk," Sam said when I finished whispering my sordid confession.

"I know."

"And you still think she'll help you?"

"Yes."

"And this Ellie's never found anyone else?"

"I guess not."

"Mm."

"What did that mean, Sam?"

"Never mind."

I was suddenly glad I hadn't mentioned the wedding thing.

The next morning, Sam had already gone to work and Billy and Butkis were still dead to the world on our living room couch when there was a knock at the door.

"Hi, Butch," I said, putting a note to Billy on the kitchen table. It included the recipe for Strawberry Delights. "Are we ready?"

"Almost," she said. "Put this on."

The desert-camo uniform shirt came with a matching hat that said DELTA FORCE EXTERMINATORS on it. The shirt had epaulets and a name patch on the left front pocket.

"Nicky?" I said. "I have to be Nicky?"

"Undercover work's no picnic, mister. Do you want the job or not?"

"Sorry, boss. When do we start?"

"Whenever you're ready to load up, Nicky."

Everyone's a comedian.

There was plenty of parking at the east side apartment complex. Everyone who worked for a living was already gone. We rode the elevator up and Butch rang the third-floor doorbell several times before motioning for me to play lookout while she convinced the door to be unlocked. Thomas Magnum would have been proud. What puzzled me was the fact that once inside—after electronically scanning for listening devices—the bright-eyed investigator went right to work . . . spraying for roaches.

"Why bother?" I whispered.

"If anyone walks in here," Butch said patiently, "it will look like we're exterminators, and it will *smell* like we're exterminators. Even the roaches will die, convinced beyond all doubt that we are exterminators. Pump up and work while you snoop, Nicky. You're on the clock."

Yes, boss.

I suppose the apartment had been gone over by the OPD, but it appeared as if everything was just the way Leonard Gordon left it on the day he went to work and died. On television, the P.I. always wanders around a little bit, then stumbles onto the big clue sitting neatly on the nightstand or resting, unwrinkled, on top of the wastebasket's tidy contents. Life isn't much like a tidy wastebasket; I'd have to say a commercial Dumpster more accurately fills the bill.

Big Lenny's bachelor life-style did not lend itself to neatness at all. There was no shortage of junk food, but aside from snitching a handful of pretzels, I resisted the urge to snack my way from room to room. With the green plastic sprayer balanced across my white deck shoes, I wheeled around, squirting the black rubber baseboards with Butch's nasty-smelling concoction. No one would doubt the antibug toxicity of the stuff, and I couldn't help wondering how many years it might be taking off both of our lives.

All of the wastebaskets were full. The fact that they were mostly full of food wrappers meant there wasn't much hope of a clue, but we looked anyway. Butch routinely checked the sorry-looking framed pictures on the walls, and spent a considerable amount of time in each of the apartment's closets. She too came up dry.

I circled the disheveled bedroom twice. A nasty sawed-off Ithaca 12-gauge riot gun with a black plastic pistol-grip stock stood next to the queen-sized bed, and there was a compact 9mm Beretta stuck conveniently between the mattress and box springs. The nightstand drawer held an unmarked undersized videotape, ammunition for both of the weapons, and a box of .357 ammo for the service revolver presumably now in the hands of the police. If he was a light sleeper, breaking in on a living Leonard Gordon might well have been a fatal mistake.

Prurient entertainment and home security aside, however, I found nothing resembling a clue.

"Nothing here, Nicky," Butch called from the other room. "Let's get on to the next call."

"Hey!" came the startled voice of the middle-aged woman who had just opened the apartment door. "Who are you two?"

"Delta Force Exterminators, ma'am," Butch said calmly while my heart stuck in my throat. "We have this work order from Landcaster Properties. Was this a bad time to come?"

"No," the puzzled women said, looking at the work order, "but I only called them yesterday morning to say that I wanted the dead guy's junk hauled out of here today. They've never been so punctual before!"

"Excuse me," I said, pulling the bill of my hat down slightly and avoiding the warning glance from Butch, "but did you say dead guy?"

"Sure. This is where that big slob lived who got shot over at the mall. Don't you read the news?"

"Well," I said, "now that you mention it, I guess I did read something about that."

"I should think you would," the woman huffed. "That nice reporter, Stick Foster, is a cripple just like you. Best writer the Orlando paper's ever had."

"Oh," I said while Butch's neck turned red, "is he in a chair? Small world. What's going to happen to all this stuff anyway? Did the man have family?"

"No one who'd own up and come forward," she said, flattening her apron with her hands. "I'm the building manager, and I've been authorized to give everything to the Salvation Army to hold till probate. The truck's just pulled up out front . . . oh, I'd better go show them where to come."

The woman was gone in a flash, and Butch promptly dropped her sprayer and ran into Big Lenny's bedroom.

"That was a dumb stunt, Nicky. Funny, but dumb." Her voice barely preceded her back into the front room. "Here," she said, dropping the 9mm into my pack. "It's yours."

In her other hand was the 12-gauge Ithaca pump, and under her arm was Lenny's bedside supply of ammo and the unmarked videotape I had passed over as pornographic. With dizzying speed, Butch soon had the riot gun broken down into a dozen smaller pieces and was busy stashing the parts and the ammo all over both of us. Naturally, I got the brunt of it. My backpack filled up first, then Butch made me lift myself off the wheelchair seat while she shoved the pistol-grip stock under my black, nylon-covered, one-inch foam cushion. Needless to say, I knew my hemorrhoids wouldn't care much for the additional attention.

Seconds later, with the sounds of men and hand trucks coming down the hallway toward us, Butch was left with only the gun's eighteen-inch barrel. I was too startled by it all to help or object, but she was obviously used to thinking on her feet. Inspiration suddenly struck, and she knelt at my feet, jerked up the left pant leg of my white Sears painter specials, and rammed the black metal tube up to my knee before sticking the business end in my sock and yanking the pant leg back down.

"Hi, guys," she said, meeting the movers as they turned into the doorway. "We're done in here. We'll just get out of your way. Sorry for the smell."

"It's okay," the man closest to her said as we moved past him. He was staring at her eyes, but then most men do. "Bug spray smells better than some of the people smells we get."

When you live in a wheelchair, there's just something about having a pound of lumpy plastic gun stock up your butt that doesn't sit well. I struggled to keep my balance as I pushed the considerably heavier ultralight folder down the hall and into the elevator.

"Are you nuts?" I said when the doors closed. "That was a crime!"

"The breaking and entering? It was *your* idea."

"No, you crazy stud-muffin, stealing the guy's guns!"

"I think you're a little confused there, Stick," Butch said, placing one hand on my shoulder. "Christmas is coming up in a few months, and think about how dangerous those Salvation Army guys are when they only have bells. Giving them firearms . . . now *that* would be a crime."

▽

29

I SAT NEXT to Butch in the rough-riding Blazer and tried to follow her shotgun reassembly instructions. Thankful for the vehicle's safety shoulder strap, I juggled the various plugs, pins, tubes, and springs, until they began to at least look something like they had before. Whether the gun would be functional was another matter.

"You sure impressed me with that phony work order, Butch. Do you always cover your butt like that?"

"Always."

"Mm. And why'd you snatch that videotape?" I said between bumps. "You and Todd aren't into sleaze, I hope."

"Get real, Stick. No, I figured it was trash too, but then it occurred to me that: one, old Lenny didn't have a VCR anywhere in the apartment, and two, if he had, it would probably have been VHS size. Nobody but industrial-security types use the smaller format any more."

"You mean, like the Palmetto Plaza Mall?"

"I'll make a real investigator out of you yet, Stick."

"Maybe. Where can we look at it?"

"Besides the mall? I'm not sure, but I think I know a couple of people who might have the right equipment."

I opened the box of double aught–buck shotgun shells and pulled one out to inspect it more closely. "These pretty deadly?" I asked.

"*Very* deadly at close range," Butch said. "Not a lot of pellets, maybe nine or ten, but they're big, and they pack a lot of wallop. I prefer number-four-size shot for home defense. Eighteen or nineteen times the number of pellets, so it's harder to miss, and still more than enough punch to discourage any intruder."

"You learn something new every da . . . whoa!"

We hit the pothole doing about 45 miles per hour, and shotgun shells sprang out of the cardboard box in my left hand like confetti out of David Letterman's cannons. I tried to catch them as they scattered across the front seat and the floor, but the effort was wasted. As I gathered up and replaced the first few shells, I noticed something in the bottom of the nearly empty box.

"Hello!"

"Whatcha got, Stick?"

"A SunBank card," I said, holding up the orange bank machine key.

"Too bad we don't have the PIN code number!"

"We do," I said. "Leave it to Big Lenny to write it on the card so he wouldn't have to remember it!"

"Bright guy," Butch said. "Hard number?"

"Yeah," I said with a laugh. "One, two, three, four."

"You're kidding?"

"Nope. Let's go try it out."

"You got it. Where's the nearest SunBank?"

"Semoran and University. Turn north here."

The card accessed a regular savings account, but there was nothing regular about the balance figure that appeared on the small computer screen when Butch selected "Inquiry" from the menu.

"Where does a mall security guard get a hundred grand?" I asked Butch in utter disbelief.

"The lottery?"

"Would have been in the paper," I said.

"Shrewd financial investment?"

"Right."

"That sort of leaves theft or some sort of scam, doesn't it?

I wonder whether the money was deposited over time, or in one big chunk."

"Good thought," I said. "How do we find that out?"

"Why not just ask?"

I knew that.

I read Butch the telephone number on the back of the card, and she soon had a diligent but overworked bank employee on the other end of her car's cellular connection.

"Hello? Yes, this is Mrs. Gordon. Lenny lost his last deposit slip, and I need the dates and the amounts for the month's accounting. Could you possibly save me a trip down there? Oh, thank you! The account number is 04015844208. That's right. Oh, sure. The PIN is one, two, three, four."

Butch shrugged and gave me her "apparently it's no sweat" look, and after a moment, she thanked the person on the other end of the line and disconnected.

"Our boy opened this account on the first of the month. One fat guy, one fat lump . . . a hundred thousand dollars."

"Three weeks after my wedding. Just over a week before he was shot. Mm. What if the person who gave him the money also gave him the ten-millimeter surprise!"

"It's possible, I suppose," Butch said. "But why?"

"I don't know. Blackmail?"

"Curiouser and curiouser."

No kidding.

"What is this? Stuff off one of those scrambled cable channels?"

Billy watched with a wrinkled brow while Butch's friend played with her machine's tracking adjustment, to no avail. I'd lost the bug-guy look, left Sam a note, and picked up Billy (he'd been busy trying to wash a crust of white icing off his face), before following Butch to Melbourne.

"No," I said. "It's not that, Billy, but keep guessing."

"Well, Bice?" Butch said. "Is that as good as it gets?"

"I'm afraid so," the electronics wizardess answered. "The equipment this was shot with and the player it's supposed to be seen on are probably both screwed up, by normal standards. But if they're in sync with each other, nobody'd care."

Bice. It had to be a Colorado name, or maybe something from up in the neuvo northwest. Bice Wathen played shortstop on Butch's softball team and owned a high-end stereo and electronics shop in south Melbourne, less than a mile from where my former home had been blown up and subsequently rebuilt. She did all the shop's repair work herself. Even more than Butch Grady, Bice Wathen was a startlingly healthy-looking woman. She was attractive, not as tall or as blond as Butch, but something about her suggested that she would live forever and continue to look exactly as she did on this day . . . regardless of whether she ever ate any fiber or not.

"Bice," I said, trying out the unusual name and enjoying the way it felt coming out across my teeth, "would you mind if I looked at it again?"

"Not at all, but I don't think I can stand watching it anymore . . . gives me a headache. I'll be out front if you need me. Stay as long as you like."

"Thanks."

When the tape stopped rewinding, I hit the Play button and called in my troops.

"Okay, Billy, Butch, we know the where; let's work on the who and the when."

They looked at each other with obviously puzzled expressions, decided I was nuts, and turned back, preparing to tell me as much.

"Come on," I said before they could say anything we'd all regret. "Don't tell me you didn't recognize what we're looking at? I'm ashamed of you guys."

Their eyes returned to the monitor, a stuttering mass of long, pulsating, static-filled lines and ill-defined ghostly shapes. Mostly, the dancing lines gyrated from top to bottom as the tape rolled forward, but occasionally a particularly bad electronic spasm sent them running away in all directions at once. Through it all, the facts—if somewhat surrealistic—were plain enough.

"Don't try to focus so hard," I said. "Just look at the outline, the basic shapes."

My advice didn't seem to be helping.

"It's a security camera, Butch. Think about it."

"Okay, so it's your mall," she said shortly. "Where? It's just garbage."

"Jeez, no!" Billy said, jumping up and pointing. "It's that planter by the snooty clothes store! Why didn't you tell me this was the mall? Look, there's the big bench, that's the tree, and this lighter part is the opening to the store! I'm right, huh, Stick?"

"Right on, Brother Bill. Testify!"

"Look," he said tugging Butch's sleeve and pulling her farther away from the dizzying screen. "This is the bench, here. And this—hey!—what was that?"

"People," Butch said quietly.

"People! Yeah, people going by in the mall! Jeez!"

Billy was beside himself, caught up in the thrill of the hunt. Butch, however, was not so easily vaulted to euphoria.

"So what? You know which camera shot this stuff. Big deal."

"More people! People on the bench! I can almost tell who they are!" Billy shouted, oblivious to Butch's nay-saying.

"Okay, Stick," Butch went on, "so it's a day at the mall. What does this have to do with anything?"

"Lots, I hope. That planter is where that Viper punk claimed to have hidden a stash of drugs. Maybe the same drugs that killed Martha Galliger. This tape will eventually tell us who, but we also need something to establish the when."

Butch Grady's left eyebrow rose sharply, and I love it when she does that.

"People getting up from the bench!" Billy blurted out, his enthusiasm unabated. "Going in the store! More people going by . . . look!"

"And that store just happens to be where my runaway mystery man worked," I said, trying to keep Butch's eyebrow cocked. I succeeded. "And, if this is the right day, I'd be willing to bet that somebody in these lousy pictures picked up those drugs."

"More people! Going by, coming out of the store, sure, you can almost count 'em!"

"And our late friend and armaments benefactor got it all on film," Butch said with a whistling exhalation as her punctuation. "What do you know about that?"

Not nearly enough.

"Me! Look, it's me! That's my hat! Hey guys, look . . ."

Bingo.

▽

30

THE RED LIGHT on my car phone was blinking when Billy and I got back to the car. I'd missed calls from Sam, Peter Stilles, and Stanley Fredericks. It occurred to me then that I hadn't yet returned Ellie Algretto's call. It's amazing how the human mind can selectively block out items that are apt to prove painful. I decided to call Sam at work first.

"Sorry about last night," she said.

"No sweat," I reassured her. "Besides, Billy's already coached me on how to deal with this kind of girl stuff." I winked at my embarrassed passenger, who was busy shushing me with one finger against his lips.

"He what? Never mind; I don't want to know. I called earlier to tell you that we're working late," she said. "You and Billy are on your own."

"And on your night to cook," I said. "Isn't that just *soooo* convenient?"

"Tough luck. Oh, and Peter's been trying to reach you. Have you talked to him yet?"

"No, but maybe Billy and I'll grab some fast food and go eat aboard the SS *Deathtrap*. We're only a mile away."

There was, I thought, an unusually long pause before Sam spoke again.

"What about *her*? Have you called *her* back yet?"

"Ah, well, no, not yet. Thanks for reminding me, though."

"Good-bye!"

Yikes.

Stanley had not-for-telephone news, but when I told him I was in Melbourne, he said it would keep and agreed to meet me for lunch the next day at the mall. Peter hadn't eaten, was anxious to take a break from sanding and caulking, and heartily invited us to come bearing the take-out food of our choice. "Anything," he insisted, "*except* seafood."

"So, while they aren't generally party animals," Peter said between bites of General Tsao chicken, "if you want information—especially long-ago-filed information—ask an archivist."

The old yacht rocked gently against its mooring lines, and I grudgingly had to admit that Peter was really doing a great restoration job. The decks and gunwale rails had been well sanded and covered with several coats of spar varnish; they looked very nearly new. The wheelhouse rehab was nearly complete and both teak and brass glistened in the fading light. Still, I was glad we were tied to the marina's sturdy cleats.

"So. What did you and your dusty archivist friends discover?" I said, taking Peter's bait.

"Well, it's all computers, Stick. You can go almost anywhere by computer."

"Like in the net!" Billy said. "You know, in the cyberpunk stuff like William Gibson writes."

"Exactly!" Peter said. "I loved *Mona Lisa Overdrive*. Anyway, we looked for your friend, Ernest Boyle, in a *lot* of places."

"Soda Speak?" Billy said, jumping in again and giving me his best puzzled look. "You think Soda Speak killed Big Lenny?"

"No, I don't, but we're just checking out as many possibilities as we can." I mentally kicked myself for allowing Billy to hear that, but some other sense made me want to include him. "Whatever else you hear stays between us, Billy. You got that?"

"Yeah, sure."

We both looked back at Captain Peter.

"Okay," he went on, "so it turns out that your Green Beret, *Sergeant* Boyle, was a real war hero. Commendations out the wazoo. His record reads like Sergeants York and Rock all rolled into one. I think he must have saved half the guys he served with at one time or another. His specialties were engineering, demolition, and small arms.

"Some of this stuff comes from semiaccessible military records," Peter went on, "and some of it comes from newspaper and periodical scans. The rest, I've been assured, we don't want to know where it's from. Anyway, in nineteen seventy-four Sergeant Boyle was dishonorably discharged from the U.S. Army. It was pretty hushed up, but he supposedly fragged a first louey."

"Fragged? What's fragged?" Billy asked, his eyes wide with the drama of Peter's story about a janitor he thought he knew pretty well.

"Murdered," I said. "It means to kill a superior officer. Usually it's done to look like a combat accident, but some guys who think their officer is going to get them killed just toss a grenade into his tent in the middle of the night."

"Soda Speak did *that?*" Billy was incredulous, and for good reason. "That's totally bogus!"

"I don't know, Billy," I said. "But if there'd been any real evidence against him, I think Ernest would be a janitor at Leavenworth instead of the Palmetto Plaza Mall. Anything else, Peter?"

"Only that he made some news by denying any part in the fragging and then refusing to give further testimony. And you're right, apparently they couldn't convict him on the fragging, then had no choice but to discharge him when he refused the order to answer the military court's questions."

"Mm. How's the Chinese burrito, Billy?" He sat, hanging on our every word, holding a half-eaten and totally forgotten moo shoo pork roll gingerly in his hands.

"Huh? Oh, okay," he said, coming back to the present and taking another bite. "Too many veggie things in there," he added around the new mouthful, "but it don't taste bad at all."

As I finished my own sampling of Melbourne's best Chinese take-out, I brought Peter up to date on my hit-and-miss investigation. He agreed that the videotape, once we were able to see it clearly, would likely point to both Martha Galliger's and Leonard Gordon's killer—assuming, of course, that my blackmail theory was correct. If it was Fred Lucas, then it was unlikely that we'd ever hear about it again. If it was Ernest Boyle, well, that would need to be handled carefully. When someone with Ernest's training opts to resist arrest, people die.

Any of the many miscellaneous "suspects" on my broad-based list might also appear on the tape, lifting the drugs and walking on, but the whys and the wherefores of such a scenario were far too convoluted for me to imagine. It might be that Luigi Leone, for all I knew, spiked his own cup and left it for someone else to pick up. But for whom? And why? Then there was always the possibility that my pathological tale teller, Billy, was completely blocking out truth and reality while kidding himself right along with the rest of his friends and supporters.

No way.

Then there was the newest and most unpleasant question mark on the twisted landscape. While Billy played captain up in the wheelhouse, I told Peter about Ellie Algretto. In order to make him see why she might conceivably bring poison to my wedding, I had to tell him far more of the story than I would have liked.

"Boy, Stick," Peter said when I wrapped up my personal soap opera, "you sure were a jerk back then."

"Thanks, Peter. Like I don't know that."

"Sorry," he said, meaning it, "but if this Ellie really is stuck on you after all these years, wanting to kill Sam—or you for that matter—"

I reeled. The thought that I might be the target had never even crossed my cobweb-covered mind.

"—wouldn't be that uncommon a motive. But why would she put the stuff in one seemingly random paper cup?"

I wish I knew.

"I guess tomorrow will tell," I said with a shrug. "But I have this desire to figure it all out before anybody sees the film at eleven. Know what I mean?"

Peter nodded.

"Do me another favor, will you, Peter? Invite Billy to net fish with you tonight and run the traps in the morning."

"Sure. But why?"

"I want someone keeping tabs on him, just in case. I'll call you after lunch and come get him as soon as I can. Okay?"

"Sure. Hey, Captain Billy!" Peter shouted. "Come on down here a minute!"

Stanley surely knew there were some rather large holes in the story I was telling him, but the tape itself sitting there on the food court table between us distracted him from asking questions that I couldn't very well answer. He looked at it like a coon dog eyeing the critter it had just run up a tree.

"Well," he said finally, "we don't often get things handed to us quite so neatly, but I'd say we're due. You are going to give this to me, aren't you? I don't want to have to kidnap anyone."

"Right," I said with a laugh, "like ten o'clock last year at Mosquito Lagoon! Stan, that was about as boneheaded as anything either one of us has ever done."

"Heckuva story, though. Well, what about it?"

"You could always shoot me down like a dog," I said. "Or didn't they give you back your gun?"

"Very funny."

By the look in Stanley's eyes, I knew that last crack rubbed too recent a wound.

"I'm sorry, Stan. It's all yours . . . on one condition: You've got to give me your word that you'll explain it all to me when you and the OPD get it unraveled."

"Deal. Which reminds me of my news. Jody and I decided to tell you what we found out about Fred Lucas, but you can't use it and you can't tell anyone. Okay?"

"Okay."

▽

31

AS I DROVE west on Colonial Drive, I decided that I was almost ready to bet on Fred Lucas. According to Stanley, the man had been a low-level hustler, sort of a dandy with aspirations for rank and privilege within one of New York's more legendary organized-crime families. Maybe he thought moonlighting with small-scale drug and prostitution operations of his own would endear him to his superiors, or that it was an easy and harmless way to make a few extra bucks. In either case, he was wrong . . . nearly dead wrong.

To save his own skin, he agreed to turn state's witness in the racketeering and tax evasion trial of one of his former employers. Then, complete with a new hair cut and color, a pair of tinted contact lens, and a rather extensive nose job, Fred Lucas was, quite suddenly, a new man. At least on the outside. Uncle Sam also gave him a new job, a new apartment, and a lifetime stipend to ease the trauma of having his underworldly butt pulled out of the fire.

I drove into the west Orlando shopping plaza, stopped under a tree near the highway, and looked out over the parking lot as I reached for the cellular telephone. Little Oak Books sat quaintly near the corner of the long *L*-shaped row of shops. Several customers came and went while I held the phone without making any move to press its buttons. It was impulsive and illogical, certainly stupid, driving all the way out west of town just to telephone Eleanor Algretto. But wherever you go, there you are.

Hanging out with the mall rats had been a refresher course in the magic and mystery of adolescent emotions. The tumultuous passions are so volatile and so dramatic that they quickly become detrimental to maturing individuals who would fit comfortably into the society around them. They are often—as in my case—locked away where, hopefully, they will never embarrass us again. Sometimes, however, triggered by circumstances unforeseen, the old feelings come rushing back with all the intensity of youth and all the embellishments of time past.

Like most emotional matters, it took me awhile to figure out what was going on. Suspicions aside, I suddenly knew—or at least was finally willing to admit—what was happening to me. From the very moment Ellie sat down next to me I'd felt like the little Dutch boy with his finger jabbed tenuously into the hole in the dike around his town. The sound of her voice, the fragrance of her perfume, the texture of her skin, the smooth, inviting curve of her lips and of her . . .

Get a grip, Stick! Are you nuts?

Maybe. Who wants to know?

My palms were sweaty and my heart was racing. As I chided myself and struggled to regain some control of my emotions and my blood pressure, Ellie came out the front door of Little Oak Books and walked east down the sidewalk. I set down the phone. Yes, in one way she was the same girl who had filled a sixteen-year-old's dreams with love and lust. On the other hand, everything else but right and wrong had changed.

"The Lord hates every kind of cheating."

I could almost hear my father. Chapter twenty, I think.

"The character of even a child can be known by the way he acts—whether what he does is pure and right."

Okay. Okay. I freaked a little. I went away there for a minute, but I'm back now. Everything's under control; I can handle this. Except . . . I *really* wanted to see the inside of Ellie's bookstore.

I left the Oldsmobile there in the shade and crossed the

parking lot in my wheelchair. The second I rolled out from under the branches of the old oak tree, the asphalt-intensified afternoon heat surrounded me. My 90-psi Continental sew-ups made staccato snapping sounds as the soft tarmac relentlessly tried to catch and hold them in place. Unlike the dinosaurs, however, I made it through the threatening tar pit and cruised up onto the concrete sidewalk and into the shade of the overhanging roof. The smooth orange tire treads were now black, but otherwise I had survived.

Entering and surviving the forbidden bookshop was another matter. I waited until the clerk at the front register was busy ringing up a sale, and slipped through the glass door and down the nearest aisle toward the back of the store. Tinkling bells announced that the door had been opened, but if the attractive black woman looked up from her sale, she would see nothing. Sometimes it pays not to be six-foot-four anymore. But not often.

The shop had a warm, quiet, friendly atmosphere that I hoped still accurately reflected its owner's personality. The aisles were wide and the various subject sections were clearly marked by attractive custom-made signs hanging from the ceiling. At the end of the long aisle ahead, an office door stood ajar. Even without an electronic keypad on the wall or an AUTHORIZED PERSONNEL ONLY sign on the door itself, I knew this room was off-limits. I could feel it from ten feet away. It wasn't the bookstore Ellie didn't want me to see; it was her private office. Naturally, I rolled right in.

"Curiosity killed the cat" was my mother's fourth favorite cliché . . . or was it the third? I used to have a list, but I lost it in boot camp.

I sat in Ellie's office, stunned beyond words or clear thought. The ten-by-twelve room should have been decorated with ordering schedules, book posters, and paperback cover blanks. Instead, it was a wall-to-wall shrine . . . an honest-to-goodness Nick Foster Hall of Fame. Every column and every article I ever wrote was framed on those four walls. There were clippings that spanned more years than I wanted to remember, from high school athletic coverage to headlines from across the country about the NASA affair a year before.

And pictures. The occasional newspaper photo was bad enough, but there were yearbook pictures—football, basketball, and track. Then there were the snapshots Ellie's father had taken of us together.

"You!"

I thought I was going to stand up when the black woman's voice hit me from behind like a bullet between the shoulder blades.

"You don't belong in here! *Nobody* belongs in here. Dear Lord, but you're pure trouble," she said as she manhandled my chair around and thrust me back out onto the sales floor. The front-door bells tinkled, and the poor woman nearly came apart.

"Lord help us!" she whispered, ducking down below the shelf tops and pushing me more urgently toward the far side of the store. "She's back with the sandwiches!"

All I could do was hang on. We zigzagged recklessly across the sales floor, dodging wooden shelves and colorful cardboard paperback display racks. When it looked like we'd finally come to the end of Mr. Gimp's Wild Ride at a ceiling-high stack of book-laden wall shelves, my wide-eyed attendant spun me around faster than a Kansas tornado, swept a large black cat up into her arms, and collapsed into the Victorian high-backed wing chair upon which the startled feline had been napping peacefully.

"My name is Rachael Evans," she whispered, before shouting, "I'm back here, Eleanor!"

The frantic woman crossed her legs, closed her eyes, and willed herself to relax. It worked. She stroked the cat and gave me a look that clearly meant: Play along or face the consequences. Between us stood an antique lamp stand serving as a book table upon which, along with several ancient volumes, was an expensive-looking silver tea service. It was only as Ellie appeared between the bookshelves near mid-store, with a bright blue-and-yellow bag from Substantial Subs, that I realized the wooden sign hanging like Damocles's sword over my head said "MYSTERY."

"You!"

Here we go again.

"I *asked* you not to come here!"

"I know, but I—"

"And you just march in here as if you never heard me."

"I didn't actually *march*—"

"Why? I've never asked you for anything. Why couldn't you just do me that one small courtesy?"

Ouch.

"It's my fault," the fully composed-looking Ms. Evans said. "I asked him to sit and wait for you. I've never met a famous newspaper writer before. I'm sorry if I did something wrong."

God bless compassionate women. Keep and protect them from nice guys and jerks.

"Oh, no, Rachael!" Ellie said, as if noticing her salesclerk for the first time. "It's nothing you did. Never mind."

With an unsettled glance toward the far back corner of her shop, Ellie handed Rachael a foil-covered sandwich and a soft drink before crossing in front of me to the matching wingback chair and sitting down.

"I don't know, Nick," she said, unwrapping her own lunch. "Maybe I'm just being silly. Here, take half. It's roast beef on sourdough. Your favorite."

"I, uh . . . thanks." I took the offering and the napkin and, because I could think of nothing sensible to say, I took a bite designed to give me enough time to settle myself down.

The bells sounded again, and Rachael rose gracefully, replaced the purring black cat to its throne with several loving strokes down the length of its back, and gathered up her lunch.

"I'll finish this up front, Eleanor, where I can tend to the register. You just take your time." Ellie nodded to Rachael, and Rachael nodded to me. "It was nice talking with you, Mr. Foster. I hope we can chat again sometime."

Right.

"Call me Stick," I said as she turned and walked away. Okay, so it was the second thing that came to mind.

I decided to chew my second bite a little longer, even though I couldn't taste it at all. Ellie's perfume was filling my fuzzy head with images best left unseen and unremembered. She just sat there watching me while she chewed, dressed in brown huarache sandals, beige slacks, and a peach-colored silk blouse that told me too much about her.

"Sam told me you called," I said with my mouth still partially full. Saying Sam's name out loud helped restore some stability to my wavering thought process.

"I'll bet she did."

Meow Mix, anyone?

When she was finally ready to get down to business, Ellie demurely touched her napkin to her lips, used it to brush several stray lettuce shreds out of my beard, and then broke the awkward silence with a vengeance.

"I know who killed Martha Galliger."

Of all the things I had imagined she might say to me, that wasn't on the list.

"It's as plain as the beard on your face, Nick. I suspected as much even before talking to Daddy. Now I'm sure of it. It was her sister."

I was about to interrupt and bring her up to date on Fred Lucas, Ernest Boyle, and the videotape—items that I obviously could not include in my newspaper column—but something caused me to hold my tongue. And yes, I know I should pay attention to those somethings more often.

"Constance was a wild one, Nick. According to the old-timers in the CGA, Wilfred Galliger spent a fortune trying to keep his youngest daughter out of jail. She blew up mailboxes, shot out people's windows, and stole anything that wasn't nailed down. And the sisters *never* got along. Not before the old man died. Not after. Wilfred gave Martha all the authority *and* all the money. According to Daddy, only Constance's marriage or Martha's death would allow Constance to receive her portion of the estate. It's the classic murder," Ellie said lightly, waving her left hand at the wall of books beside her. "Motive and opportunity . . . neat as you please."

▽

32

"OKAY, STAN," I said to myself as I parked the car and picked up the cellular phone. "I give up. I'm sitting down, ready for the sixty-four-thousand-dollar answer."

It took me the entire drive back to the Palmetto Plaza Mall to recover from my bizarre visit to Little Oak Books. Not having time to reflect on it properly while it was happening probably got me through my perplexing chat with Ellie, but once outside, the ramifications of everything I'd seen and heard took some serious sorting out. Visions of her office kept coming back to me, and I found myself contemplating the thin line between love, obsession, and possession.

And the notion that Constance Galliger might have killed her older sister was certainly not a new one. For the first week or so, everyone official—from the police to the life insurance carriers to the Galliger estate managers—worked on that obvious assumption and set it aside with satisfaction reflected in the millions. The troubling thing about hearing Eleanor Algretto put forward the old theory was the exuberance and the intensity of her sales pitch. She desperately wanted to convince me; and when I left, I felt certain that she thought she had succeeded.

It occurred to me as I drove away from the bookshop that Ellie never answered my original question about the degree of dislike present members of the Citrus Growers Association might have harbored against Martha Galliger. I decided to go right to the source and called the bookstore, hoping Rachael Evans would answer the phone. When she did, I thanked her for rescuing me from my own lack of common sense, asked her not to mention that I had called, and requested Armand Algretto's home number.

"I don't have that here," she whispered, "but then he and Mrs. Algretto have been in Europe for almost a month."

Mm.

So, as I sat in the mall parking lot, neither Fred Lucas nor Ernest Boyle had a lock on this election. There were still ballots to be counted. If Stan told me that Eleanor Algretto was the star of Big Lenny's totally hidden videotape, I wouldn't be nearly as surprised as if I had seen it myself at Bice Wathen's shop the day before. Still, I thought it unlikely . . . or at least I wanted to.

"Agent Fredericks. How may I help you?"

"I want world peace and pepperoni pizza. Can you do that?"

"I'm sorry, but that's the FBI's Hump Day Special, available on Wednesdays only. What's up, Stick?"

"I'm throwing in the towel, Stan. I wanted to figure this thing out before you guys ran the videotape, but now I've got more suspects than ever. So let's get it over with. What's the tale of the tape?"

"Well," Stanley answered, with a stretched-out pronunciation that made *well* sound like a three-syllable word, "we've got just a little problem there."

"What problem, Stanley? You promised you'd tell me as soon as you knew."

"I know, and I will. It's just that the folks at the crime lab are having a little more difficulty with the tape then they expected."

"A little more difficulty?"

"Okay, a lot of difficulty. They couldn't make heads nor tails of it."

"Well, shoot, Stan," I said, exasperated at our tireless but sometimes uninspired civil servants, "just bring it down here to the mall and we'll run it on the equipment that created it in the first place."

"Well," he said, with yet another syllable added, "I suggested that earlier, but they wouldn't hear of it. Sort of a pride and honor within the department thing, I think. Anyway, I was going to go over their heads, but then there've been a couple of additional complications that prevent us from taking that course of action at this time."

"Stan, would you cut the bureaucratic bull and tell me what happened to the tape?"

"Relax, it's just couple of breaks here and there and a few tangles. Nothing a little time and TLC can't fix."

Wouldn't you know it?

"Thanks, Stan. I knew I could count on the professionals."

I called Peter next, arranged to get my mall rat back, and offered to take them out for pizza. Peter said they'd be ready whenever I got there. Sam was next, and she too accepted my invitation. While I was at it, I called Todd and Butch. Then I got caught up in the generous (but mischievous) host routine and made one more call.

"Hello?"

"Hi. This is Stick Foster. A bunch of us are getting together at the Melbourne Pizza Den later. Would you care to join us? My treat."

"Well, er . . . sure, I guess so."

Mm. Bad host.

"You what?" Sam said, as we sped east on Highway 50. "You love to ask for trouble, don't you? You just can't wait for the inevitable disaster to find you; you have to send up flares to announce your location to the universe."

"Makes life fun, I guess. Call this one of my hunches."

"When's the last time one of your hunches paid off?"

"That night about a year ago, when I called you from the lobby of Florida Hospital."

"Okay. Besides that."

"All the others pale by comparison."

"I'm going to be sick. Pull over."

Another hunch told me to do as I was told. I don't really want to know who helped Sam perfect that particular kiss, but the man gets my vote for a Nobel Prize.

We called Peter and Billy when we were about five minutes out. They pulled into the Pizza Den lot right behind us, and Billy was out of the old pickup and talking ninety miles an hour before Peter even turned off the engine.

"Man, Stick!" he said while I transferred into my wheelchair. "It was awesome! We spent most of the night out on the water, setting nets and catching mullet . . . hundreds of them! It was *so* cool! Then we did the crab traps, and took the crabs to market, and everything! And guess what? Peter offered me a job for the rest of the summer . . . room and board (that means I get to *live* on the boat!) *and* two bucks an hour when I'm working! Can I do it, huh?"

"Well," I said, glancing at Peter to make sure I was getting the steel deal. He nodded with a genuinely enthusiastic smile. "I'm not the one to say, Billy, but I will try to help you work it out with Juvey and with your mother."

"All right!"

Billy was still doing his victory dance around us in the parking lot when Todd and Butch pulled in. I didn't recall ever seeing Todd drive Butch's Blazer before. In fact, I couldn't recall ever seeing *anyone* else drive Butch's Blazer before. It must be love. We were still visiting outside when a sleek, black Porsche convertible roared past us and into the lot with its top down.

"Hey!" said Butch. "It's Bice!"

"You know *her?*" Peter said, taking Butch's arm away from Todd and ushering her toward the newcomer. "I'll give you my yacht if you introduce me."

"You were saying something about my hunches?" I whispered to my chagrined bride. She just shook her head.

Some enchanted evening . . .

Over pizza and cold drinks I brought everyone up to speed on the temporarily waylaid investigation. They got a kick out of Stanley's admission about the crime lab's screwup, and I tried not to seem overly concerned as I recounted my strange visit to Little Oak Books, but everyone at the round plaid plastic-covered table reacted with considerable alarm. Sam stiffened visibly.

"Let me get this straight," she said. "First this crazy woman crashes our wedding, then you go out there for a friendly visit . . . *twice*?"

Oops.

"Well," I said, "I don't know. I just kept thinking I was misreading the signals; you know, it's flattering and all that, kind of a boost to the old ego that Ellie would still be hung up on me, but it just seemed so unlikely. What I *really* wanted to see was the store . . . just because she said I couldn't."

"Why'd you ask her for help in the first place if things went so badly between you?" Bice asked.

"Her dad's the only other person I know, even remotely, who's a member of the CGA . . . well, besides Constance Galliger, I guess."

The debate was long and lively about who it would ultimately turn out to be picking up the drugs on Big Lenny's videotape. Votes were cast, withdrawn, and recast as various theories were expanded and/or embellished. In the end, even though I insisted it was possible but unlikely, Eleanor Algretto was the heavy favorite. There was no question where Sam stood on the matter.

"She's bad news, Stick," Butch said to me as we left. "Be careful."

"I agree, Stick," Todd said. "It's just too creepy. What's it been, nine or ten years? That's a long crush."

"That's no crush," Bice said seriously. "That's more like a fatal attraction."

▽

33

BILLY FELL ASLEEP on Sam's shoulder before we crossed the Melbourne city limits. It didn't help matters that he smelled of mullet and dead crabs, but I knew Sam was far more concerned about something else at the moment. I also knew that I wasn't going to bring it up.

As we left the impromptu party, I overheard Peter telling Bice about the old yacht he was restoring, suavely suggesting that she might come by and give him some ideas about installing a good stereo system. Even after having lived with Peter for almost six months, I'm still surprised by him sometimes. Bice was a bright young woman who, according to Butch, had all but despaired of finding a sensitive, intelligent guy who could carry on a conversation about something besides sports and beer. Bice could pretty much pick her subject with Peter Stilles; I'd certainly never found a topic about which he couldn't hold up his end of a conversation. And yet, somehow, he never came off as a geek.

"We need to talk," Sam said quietly.

I need full shields *now*, Mr. Scott!

We've not got the power, Captain! I need more time!

Scotty, we're all out of time. . . .

"Sure," I said carefully.

"Are you having second thoughts?"

Belay that order, Mr. Scott.

Aye, Captain.

"About what?"

"About us."

"Sam, it's like this," I said, feeling solid inside for the first time in days. "I don't know why you fell for me in the first place, and I still can't believe you married me, but the only second thoughts I have about us have to do with how often I can have seconds of everything you do to me."

"Stick?"

"What now?"

"Drive faster."

Yes, ma'am.

Billy was scrubbed, groomed, and dressed in a new pair of Levi's and a Ron Jon long-sleeved T-shirt when Sam brought him to the meeting at Juvey the next afternoon. I wasn't surprised that she'd agreed to take him for a shopping spree—after all, it was her big chance to be rid of him—but the Nike Air Jordans nearly moved me to tears. The kid actually got to her. Way to go, bud!

Stanley was already there when I arrived. He had nodded a greeting but continued his discussion with someone I guessed was a detective from the OPD. She didn't seem totally sold on whatever it was Stan was hawking, but she listened intently.

Peter walked in a few minutes later, accompanied by a healthy-looking Melbourne Chamber of Commerce member who would presumably act as a character witness should one be requested. Everyone was seated and taking uneasy glances at their watches by the time Mrs. Simpson finally floundered into the conference room, apologizing profusely for any number of unrelated things. I waited for Billy to express his embarrassment, but the boy surprised me again.

"Hey, Mom!" he said, waving to her as an Orange County youth counselor ushered her warily to a chair. "Guess what? I've got a real job, and I get to sleep on a yacht, and look . . . Air Jordans!"

Okay, so he actually put his foot on the table. It seemed to me at the time that since the sneakers were easily worth fifty bucks more than the table, any reasonable person would understand. The three county employees seemed pleased by the boy's exuberance, and one of them opened the meeting by announcing that the Palmetto Plaza Mall owners had been persuaded not to press charges against him.

Yes!

"The matter of Agent Fredericks's gun," the youth worker went on, "and the murder of Leonard Gordon remain concerns. We've read your request, Mr. Foster, and we appreciate the obvious benefits to all concerned. We will, however, require consent from both Mrs. Simpson and the law enforcement departments involved before presenting this proposal to the judge for her approval. Mrs. Simpson?"

"Um, I'm sorry. What did you say? I didn't sleep well last night—"

"It's all right, Mrs. Simpson. We'd just like to know if Billy has your permission to live and work with Mr. Stilles for the rest of the summer. If he does have your permission, we'd like you to sign a brief statement to that effect."

The idea of Billy needing her permission for anything was obviously a new concept to his mother. She straightened in her chair, figuratively arranging the mantle of authority she had long since despaired of wearing again. I prayed that the power would not go directly to her already overburdened head.

"Why are you doing this?" she said, turning suddenly to Peter.

"Because I can use a good first mate, Mrs. Simpson," he answered with a natural smile. "And because Billy's a hard worker and we make a good team."

This clearly set the poor woman back a bit, but Peter turned to the three county youth workers and went on. "I also think I can help Billy get caught up a little before school starts. Especially in math. He's already shown an interest in my computer system, and learned how to enter my daily business records on a spread sheet program in ten minutes' time."

"Peter knows about everything, Mom," Billy said with feeling. "And he's a great guy, just like Stick and Sam. Please!

It'd be even better than the summer camps we've always talked about, because I'd get paid."

Nice touch, bud.

In the end, just having the power again—even for a moment—proved to be enough. Underneath Mrs. Simpson's beleaguered appearance beat the heart of a struggling mother who sincerely wanted the best for her son. If the county felt that the plan was in Billy's best interest, she agreed to give her permission.

"Way to go, Mom!" Billy burst out. "Most excellent!"

The Orlando Police Department proved to be less willing to allow their prime murder suspect to leave the county . . . at least until they'd had a clear look at the videotape. At the rate they were going, that could be some time yet. Stanley, however, attacked the situation with a startling demonstration that gave everyone pause.

"Bill," he said, standing up and walking over to the telephone in the corner of the conference room, "have you ever fired a pistol?"

"No . . . but I'd like to!"

Down, boy.

"Most young men would," Stan said as he retrieved both the Orlando residential and business directories from the shelf under the phone table. "I sure remember my first time."

He carried the thick phone books over to the ragged Naugahyde sofa at the far end of the room and placed them upright, back to back, with two of the sofa cushions stacked behind them.

"Well, Bill, you read lots of comics about guns, don't you?" Stanley asked calmly, as he pulled a replacement 10mm service automatic from its holster. "I mean, you'd know *how* to fire a pistol, wouldn't you?"

"Yeah, sure! You bet!" Billy said, practically floating out of the chair between Sam's and my own.

Stanley, whose side are you on here, anyway? Nothing like giving the boy a rope with a loop already tied in one end. I tried desperately to think of an even greater catastrophe I might unleash, one that could perhaps waylay the one Stanley was orchestrating on Billy's behalf.

"I thought so. Come here a second."

The man had done some pretty nutty things in the line of duty—and they usually proved disastrous—but he'd always acted with the best of intentions. If I was struggling to give him the benefit of the doubt, the others present were clearly becoming unnerved. There was some furtive throat clearing, maybe a mumble or two, but aside from a general exodus away from the table and toward the opposite end of the conference room, no one acted to intervene.

"Here are some foam earplugs," he said handing what looked like a pair of white cigarette filters to the excited boy. "We always use ear protection at the shooting range." He took a set for himself and threw the package to his restless audience, motioning for us to follow suit.

"Is this man's graphic equalizer running a few megahertz short of the full range," Bice whispered to Peter as she stuffed foam rubber in her ears, "or is it just me?"

"How would I know? Stick? He's your friend."

All I could do was shrug helplessly and watch with a growing sense of dismay.

"Here you go, Bill," Stan said, handing Billy the weapon and moving him several feet closer to the sofa. "Let's see you put one right in the middle of that phone book."

"All right!" Billy said, spinning around to make sure I was watching. The three county workers fell gasping to the floor as the weapon followed the boy around and passed across each of their chests. "Watch this!"

Billy took a two-handed combat stance he had surely seen many times in his comics and in the movies he loved. He pulled a bead on the makeshift target, squeezed his eyes tightly shut, and jerked vainly on the trigger.

"Wait! Wait!" he said. "I know this! There's a safety somewhere. Wait. Give me another chance. . . ."

He studied the weapon closely before finding what he sought.

"Here! I've got it . . . wait!"

When he pushed against the side of the pistol, the ammunition magazine dropped neatly out of the gun's hollow grip and bounced on the floor at his feet.

"Jeez! Sorry," he said, sweeping up the magazine and fumbling with it for several seconds before managing to get it secured back in its place. "Just a minute, please. . . ."

When he eventually found and released the safety, Billy went back into his attack stance, pointed the gun at the phone books, and closed his eyes. The loud but impotent click made everyone jump . . . including Billy.

"No fair!" he said, looking up at Stanley. "It's a trick. The gun's broken, so I can't really fire it at all, can I?"

"Well, Billy," Stan said as he took his weapon and yanked the slide mechanism back hard before releasing it with a snap, "it is sort of a trick."

He pointed casually at the sofa and the explosion that followed seemed to rock the room and everyone in it, but poor Billy nearly came out of his skin. There's nothing quite like the sound of a large-bore handgun fired in a closed room to drive home a message. The front of the leading phone book was blackened by unburned powder but was otherwise unscathed. A blank.

"I concede your point, Agent Fredericks," the Orlando police detective said without rancor. "This young man obviously didn't commit a calm, cold, and calculated walk-by shooting in the middle of a crowded mall . . . and certainly not with that weapon. I'll approve the arrangement if it suits the judge."

Stan*ley!* Stan*ley!* Stan*ley!*

▽

34

THE NEXT DAY, while the mall rats threw Billy a going away party, Stanley stopped by the Palmetto Plaza to assure me that the OPD and the FBI were both taking a more serious look at some of the other suspect possibilities in the two murder cases. After I explained my blackmail theory, the OPD immediately ran down Leonard Gordon's home records. As it turns out, the Salvation Army boxed and stored Lenny's personal effects, just in case a long-lost relative or diligent estate lawyer came forward to recapture the past. I didn't ask who got the $100,000.

The videotape was still being untangled and put back together at the Orlando Crime Lab, but because there is a more or less direct relationship between dog years and government years, even Stanley wasn't holding his breath. Still, it was only a matter of time before the puzzle would be solved. The two most important things in my mind were Billy's being cleared and Constance Galliger's right to know that some significant progress had been made in the search for her sister's killer.

"It must be hard for someone like Constance," I said to Stanley. "You know, always wondering what happened and coming, in time, to believe that no one else really cares."

"It's not that the police don't care. It's just that too many murderers leave too few clues. Even in this case, Stick, we'll all probably know who walked off with that stash of drugs when the videotape is fixed, and as logical as your theory about the blackmail and the shooting seems to be, we have no witness to say who actually put the drugs in Miss Martha's cup, or who lifted my gun, or even who used it to shoot Leonard Gordon."

"That stinks," I said, realizing for the first time how much and how little the tape would really tell us. "Does this happen often?"

"Most of the time. That's why so many criminals walk away when everyone including the judge and the jury believes they're guilty."

At least I'd knew it *wasn't* Billy. That counted for a lot. And the more I thought about it, the more I realized I wanted Constance Galliger to know that he was innocent too. Regardless of who actually killed her sister, she should be aware that the kid she had so hastily accused of the murder—just because he was a mall rat—had nothing whatsoever to do with it . . . both for Billy's sake and for her own.

So, before Billy and I left for Melbourne, we drove out to the big white house on Fish Lake. I called ahead and told Constance that we were coming by but wouldn't stay long. She met us in the driveway, wearing the same light shawl she had worn the first time I came out.

"About finished peeling?" she asked, looking at my nose.

"I hope so."

"I made some lemonade. Would you care to come in?"

"For just a moment or two. I'm taking Billy to Melbourne this afternoon. He starts a new summer job tonight."

Constance hesitated but finally made eye contact with the boy for the first time. She nodded her head and said, "Congratulations."

"Thanks," Billy said as Constance led us around behind the house to the kitchen door. "I get to go fishing every day, live on a yacht, and I even get paid for it!"

"Do you remember Peter Stilles?" I asked. "He was the best man at my wedding."

"Yes I do," Constance said. "He was a handsome young man, as I recall."

"He took over his brother's crab business last year, and now he's restoring an old live-on yacht. Billy's going to be his helper for the rest of the summer."

"First mate!" Billy corrected me.

"Forgive me. First mate."

"Well," Constance said as she got down three jelly glasses and set them next to the refrigerator, "I would have to guess that you didn't come all the way out here to tell me about this young man's summer employment. Am I correct?"

"You are," I said with a laugh. "No, Constance, there are two reasons for our visit. First, I wanted you to know that both the FBI and the Orlando Police Department have agreed that Billy had nothing to do with either your sister's death or the subsequent and related murder of Leonard Gordon."

"Related? What makes you think the two are related?"

"The week before he was shot, Leonard Gordon deposited one hundred thousand dollars in a new SunBank account. We're pretty sure he was blackmailing the person who poisoned your sister."

Constance placed a bowl of pretzel mix on the table. "I see. So you think this Mr. Gordon knew who killed Martha?"

"That's the other thing I came out to tell you," I said, munching as I talked. "We're just hours away from finding out who that was, and I thought you'd like to know."

"Why, thank you," she said as she took a plastic box of ice cubes from the freezer and started to place ice in the waiting glasses, "but I guess I don't follow. How is it that you expect to discover this killer's identity?"

"Leonard Gordon videotaped the drug pickup," I said. "The police are trying to get that tape cleared up even as we speak."

"Yeah," Billy added with a mouthful of the salty snack, "we both saw the tape before it went to the crime lab, and it was pretty fuzzy, but still . . ."

Billy fell quiet in mid-sentence, but I didn't turn to look at him. I was watching Constance Galliger's back. As she stirred the lemonade and then turned to serve us, she appeared pale and somehow tense.

"Are you all right?"

"I'm fine," she said stiffly. "It was so considerate of you to come tell me about all this." She straightened the delicately embroidered shawl, pulling it tighter around her shoulders as she stepped into the pantry.

"That's it! It's the shawl!" Billy said after draining half of his lemonade in one long gulp. "You and your sister are in the tape too! On the bench! Wow!"

Out of the mouths of babes. The great—but too late—light dawned on me in one instant, and Billy and I were looking down the twin barrels of Constance Galliger's 12-gauge shotgun in the next. The poor kid still didn't understand the significance of what he had just said.

"Hey! What's going on?"

"Sit very still, Billy," I said. "I think we just found out who picked those drugs out of the planter."

"We did? Oh, jeez . . ."

Constance sat down heavily at the end of the table and shook her head.

"I waited so long," she said. "Martha got everything. She told me what to do, when to do it, and how much I could spend doing it . . . right down to the penny. If I crossed her, even looked at her wrong, she'd cut me off for weeks at a time. I had nowhere to go, Mr. Foster."

"Shooting us won't do much for your options either, Constance. At least let the boy go. A jury might understand about your sister and Leonard Gordon, but they'll fry you for shooting a kid."

The woman with the shotgun actually smiled.

"You're probably right. I wish I'd met someone like you years ago, Mr. Foster. You're a little slow on the uptake, but you don't give up, I'll give you that. Between the two of us, we might have even side-stepped the old tyrant herself. Oh, two or three young gentlemen tried to court me after Father died, but Martha drove them off like afternoon showers. In fact, she threatened one poor fellow with this very scatter gun."

"I'm sorry," I said, meaning it, "but it really would be better if you let us go. The OPD has probably already screened that tape, so you have nothing to gain."

"And nothing to lose," she said with a wry smile and a glance at her watch. "The crime lab closed for the day almost an hour ago; no one's working overtime in this economy. And if they'd seen the fat man's tape, they'd have been here for me by now. I'll take care of the tape.

"You know, I never should have paid him anything in the first place," she said, shaking her head sadly. "I panicked. Hindsight is twenty-twenty, of course, but if I had it to do again, I'd arrange payment in person and shoot him down like the stupid dog that he was. Do you know what? He sneered at me when he saw me coming that day in the mall. Last arrogant and chauvinistic thought he ever had, eh?"

"I expect it was," I said. I glanced aside to see how Billy was holding up. His eyes were open, staring at the gun barrels on the table in front of us, but something was wrong; the usually excitable kid was fighting off a yawn. "Billy, you okay?"

"Yeah, Stick, but I'm kinda sleepy." He laid his head sideways on his arms. "Wake me up when you talk her into letting us go."

"He certainly has a great deal of confidence in you," Constance said with a laugh. "I think you would have made a good father, Mr. Foster. It's just Valium," she added as I touched the boy's arm and tried to wake him.

I picked up my own glass and held it to the light, hoping to see the small yellow pills lying safely in the bottom.

"Crushed," Constance said quietly. "I always meant to use it on Martha, but until you and the children were here the other day, I'd never thought about a good enough second step; you know, to finish the job."

▽

35

I WOKE UP buried in the sand. Well, not completely buried, fortunately, but enough so that I wasn't going to crawl anywhere. I was sort of on my right side, with my left arm free and my right arm only a few inches below the surface. I worked it free without much difficulty but in doing so discovered that the rest of me might as well have been set in concrete. My wheelchair sat neatly on the sand, out of reach.

I heard rustling in the direction of the Galliger home, and looked up in time to see Constance wiping away the last tractor tire prints with a palmetto frond as she backed off the beach and into the woods. The old John Deere diesel fired up at her command and carried her off to . . . where? She was a grove owner; presumably there was an equipment shed somewhere.

Billy! I twisted around the other way as much as I could and looked behind me. There he was, mostly horizontal but buried up to his chest in the sand, snoring lightly. Beside him lay the collapsible ultralight spinning rig I carried around in my trunk. It had been fully extended and looked, for all the world, like he had just been using it. So? What was going on? My mouth was dry and pasty, and the Valium hangover was passing quickly enough, but the scenario made little sense to me. Until I noticed Rufuss.

The spoiled old gator had probably been waiting for the

noisy grove tractor to depart, and now came gliding toward us across the still water, anxious to see what his mistress had left for him.

"Billy!" I said, struggling to speak around the disgusting film in my mouth and throat. "Billy, I think it's time to wake up now!"

I glanced briefly at the other houses on the lake, all of them too distant and too well enveloped in the thick central Florida flora. The sun had dropped below the treetops, and living- or dining-room lights could already be seen through the trees at several of them. In any case, they were all too far away to hear my screaming . . . or to care what Rufuss was having for dinner.

"Bill! Wake up!"

I tried to sit but had to hold myself up with my right elbow as I dug frantically around my left rib cage with my left hand.

"Billy!"

It was hopeless. The white silica beach sand Constance had so skillfully moved with the tractor would take hours to remove with one hand.

"Billy! Wake up! *Now!*"

Rufuss was halfway to the shore and seemed particularly interested in my thrashing about. Well, perhaps the old boy would be full by the time he was finished dragging me off and eating me. There was hope for Billy yet, if he'd only. . . .

"Wake up!"

I lay back and stretched toward him with my left arm. He could have touched me with his right hand if he'd been awake. In frustration and terror, I grabbed a handful of the sand and flung it at his face. Good! He reacted enough to brush the irritant off his cheeks before resuming his soft and peaceful snoring.

"Billy Simpson!" I shouted, pelting him with another handful of sand. "Wake up! Fast! Big Lenny's coming! Run!"

Rufuss climbed slowly and deliberately out of Fish Lake and into the Café de Constance. Billy, stirred from his slumber by my threats of Big Lenny, would soon wish he were being pursued by the late mall security chief.

"Huh?" he said, still mostly asleep.

"Billy! Open your eyes boy! It's me, Stick, and we're in *big* trouble. Wake up!"

I blasted him with handful after handful of sand before he opened his eyes and said, "Cut it out!"

"Good, Billy . . . now look at me. Here!"

He groggily blinked away the sleep and the sand and tried to focus on my face.

"What's going on, Stick?" he said. "And why do I have a hangover? Some party, huh?"

"Only for Rufuss if you don't get with it right now. Can you pull yourself out of the sand?"

The name Rufuss worked wonders. The mall rat immediately recognized where he was, and after a quick glance toward the approaching reptile, began squirming and digging frantically.

"Jeez, Stick! How'd you let *this* happen?"

"Bad planning, Billy. Look, forget the digging for now; it's no good. See if you can reach my fishing pole over there."

Rufuss paused, seemingly undecided as to whether he wanted an appetizer or would simply launch into the main course. When Billy stretched out toward him to retrieve the fishing rig, Rufuss made up his mind and slogged on toward the boy's movement.

"Great! Now he's coming at *me!*"

"Hey, Rufuss!" I yelled, as Billy handed me the pole, "over here!"

"I hope you have a plan," Billy said as he resumed his desperate digging.

"It's not much better than the last one," I said, turning my back to him and casting the yellow Rooster Tail out and over my wheelchair.

"Great," I heard him say. "He's still coming, in case you were wondering. Jeez, the old lady kills Big Lenny and *I'm* going to get eaten!"

I hoped maybe we could beat Rufuss off with the wheelchair, seeing as how it was either that or the tiny fiberglass fishing rod. The treble hooks caught the first time, but the chair was sitting sideways to me in the sand and the wheels would be of no use. I jerked hard but succeeded only in tipping the old folder over in the sand so that it collapsed on itself.

"He's almost here!" Billy called. "Do something fast!"

"Be still!" I said. "Maybe he'll come for me."

"No such luck. He wants mall rat. Jeez, Stick, hurry!"

The yellow fishing lure turned out to be hooked on my backpack, so when the chair fell over, the pack kept coming. The weight of it gave me hope. I snatched out my scratched-up laptop computer, twisted back to my left, and tossed it to Billy.

"Here! Try this!"

The boy caught the computer and held it up threateningly as the big gator crossed the last couple of feet between them.

"Hit him on the nose if you can," I said.

"Right," he said skeptically. He was shaking all over, and his voice was cracking, but he held himself upright and faced the monster with real moxie. "Let me know when you're ready with the real plan."

While I reached desperately for my wheelchair with my right hand, Rufuss, apparently satisfied that his prey offered no real threat, lunged forward, snapping his great jaws at the struggling boy. Billy swung nobly but missed the gator's nose by an inch. The toothy jaws came together solidly on the nine pound plastic-encased computer, which was snatched easily from Billy's hands as the reptile recoiled to study his trophy.

"He doesn't like it, Stick! Got anything else?"

Rufuss shook his head from side to side. The laptop seemed to be stuck on his teeth. I gave up on reaching my chair and unhooked the swivel snap that now connected the fishing pole to my backpack.

"Here," I said. "It's all I've got."

Billy took the pole and wielded it like a fencing foil, whipping it at the angry gator's bulbous eyes. With a mighty flip of his head and neck, Rufuss flung my poor computer fifteen feet out onto the beach behind him and turned to deal with the pesky appetizer.

I prayed for Divine intervention and grabbed the back-pack. I intended to wave it about helplessly in a desperate attempt to distract the hungry reptile, but the gaping computer pocket deposited its last remaining contents on my chest: some loose change, a blue bandanna, a copy of *Caught Looking*, and a forgotten and most excellent answer to my prayer.

The first 9mm round out of Big Lenny's bedside automatic hit well behind the gator's left eye and the second pierced his neck.

"Yes!" Billy shouted when Rufuss retreated several feet to think about his sudden headache.

I took a deep breath and put two more rounds into the creature's gnarly skull before he started rolling around wildly on the sand. The great lashing tail barely missed Billy on several occasions that the boy made a point of telling me about, but I tried to concentrate on getting another clean head shot.

"Good!" Billy shouted when I nailed Rufuss in the back of his green scaly head. "Finish him off, Stick!"

The bloody gator was still thrashing, though not as strongly, and had clearly lost all sense of where and what it was about.

"Here, Billy," I said, flicking on the weapon's safety. "You've got a better angle. Catch!"

He caught the pistol and looked at me in disbelief.

"You don't need to cock it like Agent Fredericks did. There's already a round in the chamber. Just release the safety lever, point, and squeeze. Slowly! And with your eyes open!"

Billy waited until the beast flipped its head toward him, and squeezed off a round that landed squarely between the gator's eyes. The twelve-foot monster shuddered and lay still. The boy and I glanced at each other in hopeful disbelief.

"Wow! How was that?"

"That was great, Bill. Keep an eye on him. You should have a couple of shots left if you need them."

"Can I save one for the old lady?"

"Yeah," I said with a laugh of relief, "but you can't shoot her with it."

"Bogus!"

The "old lady," as Billy had so lightheartedly pointed out, could arrive home at any moment.

▽

36

I USED THE backpack as a scoop and went back to digging myself out. Billy dug one handed for some time, keeping the small Beretta pointed at Rufuss with the other.

"Why'd you wait so long to use the gun, Stick?"

"I didn't even remember that it was in there, Bill. Butch tossed it into my pack the day we searched Big Lenny's apartment, and I just forgot about it in all the hubbub."

It was getting dark quickly, but when Billy finally decided that Rufuss was really dead and put down the pistol, he made pretty good headway. Within fifteen minutes, he'd freed himself from the sand and was busy digging down around my lifeless legs. When I was free and he had set up my wheelchair beside me, it dawned on us both that he would be unable to wheel me off the beach by himself.

"No biggie," I said, pulling off my one remaining penny loafer. "I'll scoot myself up to the driveway. You just take the wheelchair, okay?"

"Got it."

Dragging myself through the sand wasn't the easiest task in the world, but the thought that Constance might return momentarily with her shotgun kept me well motivated. Billy gathered up my battle scarred computer, shook the sand out of my backpack, and put my traveling inventory of miscellaneous stuff back in its place. Except, of course, the 9mm;

that he wore proudly, stuck in his belt at the small of his back just like Thomas Magnum. He even dug up my other shoe and placed both on the chair's seat cushion while he towed the light folder past me and up to the car.

"Call the cops from the car," I shouted as he disappeared into the woods. "Tell them to send someone here and to the crime lab."

"Got it!"

I slogged on, swinging my butt backward up the beach six or eight inches at a time, while my legs left a trail behind that looked a lot like the one Rufuss left with his tail. With every cumbersome movement, I analyzed the mystery that had very nearly gotten me eaten alive.

The shawl. It made perfect sense; in fact, I suddenly remembered seeing Constance shift it from one arm to the other the day we shook hands at Jacob's. It could easily conceal a handgun. And the white gloves! What if the stain matched the lubricant Stanley used on the 10mm that killed Big Lenny? As I pondered how she got the gun in the first place, the picture of Constance running to the pastor's study after Martha collapsed at our wedding came clearly to my mind. Boy, but I'm sure sharp as a tack when it's all over.

"They're on the way here," Billy said as he reappeared through the trees. "But there's been an explosion at the crime lab. The fire department's there and everything. Where would the crazy old bat get a bomb anyway?"

"Good question," I said, pulling myself off the beach sand and into the stand of scrub oaks and palmettos. "Ah, that's a little easier. Wait! I bet I can guess the answer to that one, Billy. Farm kids have been making bombs for generations, and unless I miss my bet, Constance used the same kind of bomb to blow up mailboxes when she was a grove rat. All she really needs is fertilizer and diesel fuel . . . she should have plenty of both around here."

"Given enough time, Mr. Foster, I believe you could think your way through a barn door."

Billy didn't even look up. He just dove headlong into the dark palmettos alongside the nearly invisible path. He was followed, immediately, by a load of buckshot that ripped up the lush flora and fauna where he had disappeared.

"Stop!" I shouted at the woman silhouetted near the driveway end of the path. "He's just a boy! Don't do this, Constance."

"I can drop her, Stick," Billy whispered from within the thick brush.

Boom!

The 12-gauge echoed over the sound of ripping vegetation.

"No! Don't do it, Billy!" I listened for the sound a double-barreled shotgun makes when it's broken open for reloading. I didn't hear it, and the silhouette didn't move. Good.

"Give it up, Constance. Come on . . . how about letting Martha go down in history as the mean sister instead of you?"

"She was the mean one," Constance whispered. "If you only knew."

"It's time to tell someone that," I said, as calmly as I could. "Someone who can help you get past it."

"After all these years being a slave and a prisoner in my own home, having to pretend on Sundays that everything was wonderful, you want me to turn myself over to a shrink . . . trade one know-it-all master for another? I don't think so, Mr. Foster."

Headlights came up the driveway behind her, making her silhouette look suddenly huge and luminescent like a partial solar eclipse. Red and blue lights flashed around the bizarre aura that was Constance Galliger, and an electronically enhanced voice called her by name and asked her to put down the gun. Instead, she turned slowly toward the lights as the voice warned her more sternly.

"No!" I shouted at the police as I scooted up the path toward her as fast as I could. "Don't shoot!"

She raised the shotgun and aimed it directly at the police cruiser.

"No!"

I wasn't going to make it.

"It's not lo . . ."

Two shots rang out, one right after the other. And Constance Galliger went down like a sack of nitrogen-rich fertilizer. Fortunately, her collapse was the result of being hit from behind by a flying mall rat, not of the police officers' warning shots.

Billy picked up the shotgun and threw it out toward the police car before helping the old woman to her feet. By the time I had climbed into my wheelchair, Constance had been read her rights and locked securely in the back of the cruiser.

"What about the crime lab?" I asked one of the officers.

"She do that too?"

"Yeah," I said, "she just got back."

"Well, you know that hideous wall sculpture on the front?"

I nodded.

"To tell you the truth, I think the city should pay her for putting it to rest."

"No kidding? That's all?"

"Oh, some brickwork," she said, "some roof repair, and a new gutter; but all in all, we think it's well worth it just to be rid of that nightmare."

Billy made arrangements to start his new job a day late, and the party I threw him at the mall the next day was more fun than I can ever remember having.

"No kidding?" Tamara said, wide-eyed as Billy told his tale.

"That means Miss Galliger must have seen you going into the vent," Jeremy pondered out loud, "or maybe just discovered it by accident. We had the scenario though, didn't we?"

My crime club worked through the mystery as Billy spoke, even to the point of speculating how Constance caught the ejected 10mm shell casing in her shawl.

"Sounds as if the old lady was, like, queen of the five-finger discount," Emily said.

"A kleptomaniac, more likely," Jeremy added. "They'll steal anything, but are sometimes not even aware that they're doing it."

The beach scene was clearly the most exciting story any of them had ever heard firsthand.

"Awesome!" Danny added. "You actually killed Rufuss yourself?"

"Like, Bart, I am *so* impressed," Emily said, watching the boy's eyes for any sign of embellishment.

"Is he jerkin' us around?" Wallace asked me.

I just shook my head and smiled.

"Fortunately for you," Jeremy interjected at one point, "the ballistic coefficient of the lead shot was not sufficient to maintain its velocity through the vegetation."

"Either that," Tamara said, rolling her eyes, "or the old church lady just missed!"

Everyone laughed.

Billy had some talent as a storyteller, and there, with the right material and no need to lie, he held the group spellbound. I made a mental note to have Peter introduce the boy to word processing. This was *Reader's Digest* stuff if I ever heard it.

I listened with greater interest when he described to them the debate he had carried on with himself, first about whether or not to shoot the dangerous church lady when he had the chance, and then whether or not to try and save her life. I had not heard before, nor do I expect to hear in the future, a more moving treatise on the value of human life.

"When she was a kid," Billy said in closing, "she was kind of like a mall rat, like us. Only she didn't have somebody like Stick around. . . ."

I don't know how that emotionally rewarding moment disintegrated into a rapping conga line around the mall food court, but I'll remember it as long as I live.

Four for the north door, five for the west,
East is six, 'cause we like that best.
We're the Palmetto Seven, and we run this ranch.
And seven is the number for Maison Blanche.